Stevie spontaneously arched her back as Jade's mouth found her left nipple, her hand closing in on and stroking Stevie's other nipple. Jade sucked gently and alternated between breasts until Stevie squirmed beneath her.

"You want more?" Jade teased, her eyebrows dancing suggestively.

Stevie was breathing hard, sweat beading on her forehead. She could only nod, her hand trailing down to her zipper, only to have Jade pull her hand away.

"That's my job," Jade answered. She tugged on Stevie's zipper, slid her hand inside Stevie's cotton boxers, her fingers becoming entangled in the web of soft hair.

"Oh, honey," Stevie breathed.

Jade pulled her hand out, much to Stevie's momentary consternation. Stevie felt she would burst at any second, and she reached for Jade's wandering hand again, aching for it to work its magic on her.

LOOKING FOR NAIAD?

**Buy our books at
www.naiadpress.com**

**or call our toll-free number
1-800-533-1973**

**or by fax (24 hours a day)
1-850-539-9731**

3rd Stevie Houston Mystery

Double Take Out

TRACEY RICHARDSON

THE NAIAD PRESS, INC.
1999

Printed in the United States of America on acid-free paper
First Edition

Editor: Lila Empson
Cover designer: Bonnie Liss (Phoenix Graphics)
Typesetter: Sandi Stancil

Library of Congress Cataloging-in-Publication Data

Richardson, Tracey.
    Double takeout : a Stevie Houston mystery / Tracey Richardson.
        p.   cm.
    ISBN 1-56280-244-5   (alk. paper)
    I. Title.
PS3568.I3195D68   1999
813'.54—dc21   98-48242
                                                                    CIP

For Sandra

Acknowledgments

My deepest thanks to my longtime partner, Sandra Green, who is always with me every step of the way. Like the character Stevie Houston, Sandra is also a police detective, but I'm afraid those who know Sandra won't find a whole lot of similarities between them. I admire Sandra's dedication to her job and her extremely high moral fiber, and I do try to model my book's heroine after Sandra in this respect.

Brenda, an ex-cop and ident expert, and a wonderful person and friend, has been a tremendous source of help to me with my novels. I'm lucky to have many supportive friends, and they have my gratitude for just being who they are.

Thanks to Naiad Press and to all those who work hard for Naiad, and thanks to my always hardworking editor, Lila Empson.

I also want to say something about the women police officers I know, who have a job not many people could or would do. They see the good, the bad, and everything in between, and somehow they manage to do their jobs with integrity, dedication, and a sense of humor. This book is also for them.

About the Author

Tracey Richardson lives in Ontario, Canada, with Sandra and their two retrievers, Cleo and Rollie. Tracey works as an editor at a daily newspaper. Her previous Stevie Houston mysteries for Naiad are *Over the Line* (1998) and *Last Rites* (1997). The romance *Northern Blue* was published in 1996. Tracey's short stories have appeared in *The Very Thought of You* (November 1999), *The Touch of Your Hand* (1998), *Lady Be Good* (1997), and *Dancing in the Dark* (1996).

PROLOGUE

The needle gleamed in direct contrast to the dull latexed hand holding it, rubbery thumb ready on the plunger.

The liquid filling the vial was clear, its purpose transparent. There was no need to swab the patch of skin with antiseptic, no need to worry about infection or the infliction of pain.

One last look at the supine figure before the needle would burst the bubble that was this man's life. Dispassionate eyes glided over the sleeping man, whose drunken haze cocooned him from his imminent

1

fate. He lay on the bed fully clothed, shirt undone, hairy stomach bubbling over like an overfilled bowl of Jell-O. His shoes were still on, the expensive Italian leather polished to a soft shine. His hair, thinning on top, was disheveled, and wisps of it feathered his lined forehead.

There were still traces of past good looks on his Pillsbury Doughboy face: the long eyelashes, a pouty bottom lip, cheekbones that were almost feminine. But these features had been nearly obliterated by years of too much food, too much drink, too many parties.

Pushing the unbuttoned sleeve up, the hand brought the needle closer. With just the slightest hesitation to locate the vein, the needle penetrated its target, the plunger driving the deadly concoction into his bloodstream.

In just a few minutes it would all be over. And Fatso would be just another underworked, overpaid, arrogant, conniving executive who'd choked on his own secret indulgences.

CHAPTER ONE

The lumbering, unmarked Chevy Caprice idled behind the double parked taxi, the one-way street too narrow and the Chevy's girth too wide for its occupants to do anything but wait.

Toronto homicide detective Stevie Houston slumped back in the driver's seat, which was sculpted soft and flat from her beefier coworkers, and made a conscious effort to be patient. She knew from living in Toronto for more than a decade that a horn blast and a tantrum would accomplish nothing. So she sighed in quiet exasperation and glanced sideways at her partner, who was one of the culprits in the pancaking of the seat.

A devilish smile spread across Stevie's strong, handsome face as she mischievously considered taking the dashboard cherry light out and lighting up this obnoxious cabby. Or maybe as soon as his fare arrived, they could hop out and make the driver take them through a spontaneous road-safety check of his vehicle, while his passenger simmered and made a mental note never to use *that* cab company again. Stevie smirked at the possibilities, anxious to share them with her partner.

She opened her mouth, looked at Ted Jovanowski again, then sighed, only this time her sigh was one of resignation. She had been partnered long enough with him now — two and a half years — to feel the weight of the sadness gathering in him, like heavy cumulo-congestus clouds, swelling and threatening in an unstable atmosphere.

Stevie felt a twitch of surprise at remembering something from a university meteorology course eons ago. Why was she suddenly thinking about storms and big gray clouds?

She dialed down the latest Jann Arden on the cheap stereo system. "You all right, Ted?"

Jovanowski reached into the breast pocket of his jacket, as he always did when something was bothering him, his fingers fishing around for an invisible cigarette. It had been more than two years since his heart attack and since he'd reluctantly quit smoking. But the urge to smoke was obviously still part of his daily routine. And that moment of realization always made him crabby.

He grunted noncommittally in response to Stevie's

question, his double chin drooping, his eyes narrowed on the taillights of the taxicab ahead. "Can't we get this fucking thing moving?"

Stevie shrugged, her annoyance with the cabby having been pushed aside by Jovanowski's surliness. "Ah, what the hell, it's a beautiful September Saturday morning, Ted. It's still better than sitting around the office waiting for something to happen."

It was their weekend on duty, and so far their plate was clean — no Friday night homicides or aggravated assaults in the city. So instead of sitting in their downtown office drinking stale coffee and forcing themselves to slog through paperwork, they'd decided to take a drive.

Jovanowski reached for the console and flicked on the siren, his other hand slamming the red dash light into place. "Maybe this'll get the asshole moving," he shouted over the shrill.

Stevie shook her head. *Great. Something's up his ass, and I'm stuck with him all weekend.*

They watched as the cabby threw his hands up in despair, as if to indicate he had no choice. Jovanowski in turn motioned him to get going. It was a standoff for a few moments until finally the frustrated driver took off with squealing tires and Stevie thankfully killed the siren.

"I'm hungry," Stevie said. "You?"

Jovanowski shrugged, staring ahead.

Stevie wheeled the car north onto Jarvis. "Something wrong, Ted?"

"Whydaya say that?"

Stevie smiled. "Because you're grouchy as hell. And when you're not interested in food, there's definitely something wrong."

5

Jovanowski grunted, looked out his passenger side window, which was rolled down.

Two years ago, Stevie would never have broached personal territory. He was gruff, cynical, and just generally grumpy as he inched closer to retirement. But Stevie and he had grown close because she'd been able to peel through the callous layers. She'd seen his sensitive side. Or rather, he'd let her see his sensitive side. And it helped that he was fond of her lover, Jade, who happened to be the city's sexiest forensic pathologist, they both agreed.

"C'mon, Ted. Is it Jocelyn?"

For over a year now, Jovanowski had been dating Joceyln Travers — a tall, attractive, forty-something solicitor general's office investigator they'd met on a case last year. They'd been to dinner at Stevie's and Jade's several times, but the last time they'd all been together — about a month ago — Stevie'd had a nagging feeling that something wasn't right.

Jovanowski sighed, his hand gliding roughly over his sandpaper chin. "It's nothing, kid. We're just taking a little time out right now, that's all."

Stevie touched his arm lightly, then wheeled the car left onto Gerrard, dodging a zealous pedestrian who obviously didn't believe in crossing with the light. "I'm sorry, Ted. Is there anything Jade or I can do?"

He shook his head and stared straight ahead, signaling an end to the conversation.

Stevie expertly maneuvered the car into a parking spot near the intersection of Yonge and Gerard and tugged her partner along to her favorite breakfast-on-the-run shop: La Maison du Croissant. Inside, she expansively breathed in the fresh aroma of flavored coffee and baking bread, and her stomach growled happily.

She ordered a fresh almond croissant and a cup of hazelnut coffee for the road and waited for Jovanowski to make up his mind. He browsed in an apathetic daze until he spied the fresh apple turnover croissants, licked his lips like the old Ted she knew, and ordered a couple.

Like the experienced cops they were, Stevie and Jovanowski skillfully balanced their coffee cups and food while driving through city traffic, letting the crumbs cascade to the seats and floor to join the rest of the stale detritus from previous occupants.

The portable telephone on the console bleeped, and Jovanowski answered it with a full mouth. He jotted down an address, and, mumbling, asked if a coroner and scenes of crime officer was there, then replaced the phone.

"What's up, Ted?"

"Fourteen-forty Roxborough Drive in Rosedale. Fifty-three division's there with a body, not sure if it's homicide or natural causes."

"Coroner there yet?" Stevie asked, pointing the car in a northerly direction.

Jovanwoski nodded. "Benton's just arrived. He'll wait for us. SOCO's not been called yet. They'll wait on our word first."

Stevie took another swallow of coffee, glad for an assignment. Even if it wasn't a homicide, it just might get her partner out of his foul mood.

From Yonge, Stevie headed east onto Carlton, past the old, yellow bricked Maple Leaf Gardens hockey arena, and made an illegal left onto Jarvis. She ignored the beeping horns and minor displays of road rage and continued north at a reasonable pace. No need to go lights and siren to a body for which there was no help now.

They were silent the rest of the way, Stevie having given up her fleeting notion of badgering Jovanowski for more on his relationship problems. Maybe she'd have more luck with Jocelyn. For although she wasn't the meddling type, Stevie knew her partner was madly in love with this woman and would probably be a sourpuss for at least the next year if they didn't patch things up.

Stevie whistled under her breath as she turned in to the driveway of the home that was now the subject of curious neighbors and humorless cops. The house was palatial, to say the least, though in a Rosedale neighborhood like this, Stevie had expected no less. Her plastic, empty coffee cup joined the rest of the litter on the floor.

The car coughed and sputtered as Stevie turned the ignition off.

"Piece of shit," Jovanowski grumbled as he pulled a large briefcase from the back seat and kicked the door shut. "You'd think they could spring for new cars every twenty years or so."

Stevie rolled her eyes and made a mental note to have a chat with Jocelyn *soon*.

A sergeant, tall and burly and who identified himself as Tim Martin, greeted them in the lobby — a ceramic-tiled and mirrored wonder — and jerked a thumb in the direction of the second floor.

"He's up in the bedroom. Dr. Benton's there too, along with one of my guys."

8

"What'd you guys touch?" Jovanowski demanded, his tone accusatory. It was just a fact of life that uniformed cops almost always arrived at a death scene before a detective or a scenes of crime officer. And what the uniforms did or didn't do at the scene could make the detective's case a nightmare or a dream.

The sergeant shook his head defensively, his eyebrows looming heavily over narrowed eyes. He puffed up his chest. "We just looked around the bedroom and upstairs bathrooms for any weapons or drugs. We did find his wallet up there, not much else."

"Well?" Jovanowski blurted impatiently. "Tell me about the wallet. And whadaya mean by 'not much else'?"

"ID confirms what his wife says. Name's James Hedley. And no signs of drugs anywhere, other than a couple of marijuana joints in the nightstand. No syringes or weapons anywhere."

"I hope to Christ you got the coroner to sign a warrant before you went nosing around," Jovanowski huffed.

The sergeant's smile was relaxed. "Of course."

"Who reported the body?" Stevie cut in as she scribbled the victim's name in her notebook and resisted the urge to roll her eyes at the exchange before her. *Male cops. Always measuring each other's dick.*

"Wife. Got the call about an hour ago." Martin glanced at his watch. "Nine A.M. She said she hadn't been home all night and came in at about seven-thirty."

"Where is she?" Stevie asked, an edge to her voice.

She was finding it hard to believe the wife had been home for ninety minutes before reporting her husband dead. She shot a quick glance at her partner.

"In the kitchen with Constable Hewitson."

"Good. Make sure she stays there until we can interview her."

Jovanowski started up the thickly carpeted stairs and began firing off questions over his shoulder, self-assured as always. His attitude on the job was simply one of superiority. He was the best, and no one should dare question his abilities or judgment. "Any money left in the wallet? Has the house been tossed? Any signs of a break-in?"

The sergeant started up the steps as well, Stevie behind him. "There's money in the wallet — couple of hundred bucks, and a couple of packaged condoms. As for the house — who can tell. There's obviously been a party here. You should see some of the rooms downstairs; they're a mess. No obvious signs of break-in."

They entered the bedroom, Jovanowski still asking questions to which the sergeant had no answers. It was Jovanowski's impatience talking more than anything. He wanted all the answers now, wanted the case solved yesterday. It was what drove him.

The body was on the bed faceup, mouth agape, still clothed. The victim, a balding chubby man, well-groomed even in death, looked as though he were sleeping mid-snore. Stevie went to the body and touched a bare forearm, which was still soft and not particularly cold.

Stevie turned her attention to the coroner, who stood near the headboard, while her partner turned his attention to their immediate surroundings.

10

"Hey, Benny," she smiled up at the tall, wiry, bespectacled young doctor who, like her, was approaching his mid-thirties. She liked him. And not because he, too, had undoubtedly danced in high school to the music of Blondie and Van Halen, but because he was sharp. And funny.

"Stevie. Bet your night wasn't half as exciting as his was," he grinned, nodding at the body.

"Just as well, I'd say." Stevie grinned back before turning serious again. "So give it to me. What do you think happened here?"

Benton stepped up to the body and held up the right arm first, then the left. Both sleeves had already been rolled up, and before Stevie could ask (as he knew she would), he told her the right sleeve was rolled up when he arrived. "There's a fresh needle mark here on the right arm inside the elbow. You can see the slight bruise. But I couldn't find any other needle marks on his arms, so he doesn't look like a regular user. From his medicine cabinet he doesn't appear to be a diabetic or anything like that, and there's no sign of drugs or syringes."

Stevie slowly nodded. "So someone's injected him with something and taken the syringe with them."

"And of course we can't know yet if what was injected was what killed him. His body smells of alcohol, so that may have been part of it."

"All right," Stevie said tersely, her mind made up. "I'm calling in scenes of crime, and we'll get a forensic autopsy."

Benton half smiled his disappointment. He would have done the autopsy had it been a natural death, but with signs of unnatural causes like this, it was a case for his forensic peers. "I understand Dr. Agawa-

Garneau is the pathologist on duty this weekend. I'll give her a call."

Stevie smiled to herself at the mention of her lover and strode briskly toward the bedroom door. "It's okay, I'll make the call as soon as I alert SOCO. Any idea how long he's been dead?"

Benton shrugged. "I haven't removed any clothing to take a rectal temp. I figured I'd wait and let the pathologist have all the fun. Rigor's not too developed, so it hasn't been long. Maybe four or five hours." He glanced at his watch. It was nearly ten-thirty.

Sitting in her unmarked car, Stevie dialed her lover's pager number from the cellular phone, left a message, then hung up. She didn't have to wait long, though it allowed her to make a few more notations in her notebook.

"Hi, honey," Stevie breathed into the handset, exhilarated by the thought of working with Jade this weekend. They'd been together for more than two years, and still Jade's voice or the sight of her made Stevie's heart catapult.

"Hey," Jade replied hurriedly, "what's up?"

Stevie could hear clattering and faint noises in the background. "You sound busy."

"Run off my feet, actually. Had a bad car accident a couple of hours ago, and we're just starting our second autopsy. One more to go after that."

Stevie winced. "Sorry to do this to you, but you'd better add another one to your list." Stevie summed up the events at 1440 Roxborough Avenue as best she could, then asked Jade if she wanted to attend the scene, as forensic pathologists often did.

Jade hesitated in contemplation, then groaned. "Shit, I really can't. I'm up to my neck here. But from what you've told me, I doubt there's anything at the scene that will help me with the cause of death. Sounds like a routine OD. I'll send a couple of transporters over. Okay, darling?"

Stevie smiled as romantic thoughts crept into her mind. "Listen, hon, I want to cook us a nice romantic dinner tonight, even if it's late."

Jade hesitated. There was more clanging in the background. "You sure you want to? I can cook something up."

Stevie laughed. "I know you're the expert cook in our household, but c'mon. I'm not *that* bad ... am I?"

Stevie nearly ran smack into Benton as he barreled out the front door.

"Is she coming over?" he asked hurriedly.

Stevie shook her head. "She's too busy, but we'll take him over as soon as our SOCO people do their thing."

"I really have to run," he said from halfway down the walk. "Couple of sudden deaths at a nursing home. They're afraid of a legionnaires' outbreak."

Stevie jogged up the stairway, suddenly irritated. She wasn't happy that neither Jade nor Benton would be able to more closely examine the body before it was taken away. Routine overdose or not, the perfectionist in her liked every inch of ground covered because a good defense lawyer would unearth even the tiniest shred of sloppiness or inattentiveness in the investigation.

Jovanowski dismissed her worries with a shrug, his mind pulsing with a mental list of the immediate things that needed to be done. Photos and videotapes had to be taken, measurements and sketches, an extensive search throughout the entire house for any evidence, fingerprints and fibers to be collected, the neighborhood to canvas for witnesses of the home's activities overnight. There was the immediate need to interview the wife, and later to come up with a list of party guests to interview. They would need to talk to the victim's friends, families, coworkers. It was a monumental, unglamorous task that could potentially take weeks of plodding, monotonous work.

Jovanowski slipped on a pair of rubber gloves. "I'll work with scenes of crime for now. Why don't you interview Mrs. Hedley?"

Stevie smiled when she saw who was in the kitchen.

Tess Hewitson beamed back. "Hey, Stevie. It's been awhile since you graced our division."

Stevie winked. Her voice dropped to a whisper. "You ever get around to asking that cute little nurse out yet that Jade keeps bugging you about?"

Tess grinned shyly, her cheeks flaming. "Not yet."

Stevie smiled, remembering how she'd taken the young cop under her wing a few months ago when Tess had come to Stevie, intent on learning how she could go about becoming a homicide dick. The two found out they had more in common than a desire to solve murders. They'd become friends.

"Where's Mrs. Hedley?" Stevie asked.

"She had to go to the washroom." Tess pointed to the half-opened door off the kitchen.

"You search it first?"

"With a fine-toothed comb," Tess answered confidently. "She's been searched too."

"Good woman." Stevie nodded her approval. The more she'd gotten to know Tess, the more she liked her chances of making homicide some day. At twenty-seven, there was still much for her to learn, and Stevie had been careful to caution her not to expect to make homicide by the age of thirty, as Stevie had.

Vanessa Hedley emerged from the washroom, her slim body rigid, her face devoid of any makeup except lipstick, her eyes as dry as her half-smile. Tess Hewitson introduced Stevie to her before taking her leave, and the two sat at the small kitchen table littered with half-empty wineglasses from the night before. A bowl of wilting flowers stood out from the mess.

"So, I guess I'm Suspect Number One," Vanessa Hedley smirked. "I'd like to call my lawyer before you take me in," she said in a voice rough and raw, like a worn-out record.

Stevie took a deep breath, not used to a primary witness — and, of course, a suspect — being in such calm control. It was up to her to take control of the interview.

Stevie's smile was threadbare, her voice even. "There's no need to take you anywhere right now, Mrs. Hedley. And what makes you think you're a suspect? No one has said your husband was murdered."

"Call me Vanessa," she answered coolly, shaking silky blond hair from her forehead. "After all, I imagine I'll be seeing a lot of you from now on. And don't try to fool me into believing my husband died of natural causes or killed himself. I saw the body. I saw the needle mark in his arm. And why else would two homicide detectives be here?"

Stevie sat back in her chair, her notebook on her lap, and took mental stock of Vanessa Hedley. She was moneyed, to be sure, confident, even arrogant. She acted as though she'd seen it all before, or at least was expecting something like this, and that it wasn't a huge concern. She was good looking, blessed with good skin and strong bones, short wavy blond hair, her eyes a clear blue, faint laugh lines around them. Late thirties, Stevie guessed, but she'd find out all the particulars later.

"You are not under arrest, Vanessa, nor are you a suspect at this time," Stevie replied. "I simply need to ask you some questions since you were the one who discovered the — your husband."

Vanessa sniffed. "And of course anything I say can be used in a court of law against me, isn't that right, Detective?"

Stevie had to grant her that, and Vanessa finally offered to answer Stevie's questions, but warned she would halt the interview at any time she felt she needed her lawyer.

Stevie began with innocuous questions about James Hedley, about their life together, who their friends were. The answers were terse, one-dimensional. After about fifteen minutes, Stevie had gone through several pages in her notebook, the most interesting notation being the one that referred to Vanessa dropping out of medical school more than a dozen years ago to marry James Hedley, a then-promising business executive.

Jovanowski popped his head through the kitchen archway and motioned for Stevie to step out into the hall with him.

"Pictures are done, and we've got a couple of guys here ready to take the body. I'm still busy here. Can you go with the body?"

Stevie shook her head. "I've got my hands full too,

16

Ted. Send Hewitson and I'll get there as soon as I can."

Stevie sat back down again and flipped to a fresh page.

"Look, Detective. I know what you're thinking." Vanessa smiled knowingly, taking a cigarette from a gold-plated case in her pocket and igniting it with a matching lighter. "You're sitting there all smug, wondering why I'm not falling apart right about now, aren't you?"

Stevie had never quite encountered anyone like this in her brief homicide career. Vanessa Hedley was smart, one who was used to games. "Yes, that's one of the things I was wondering," she answered honestly.

Vanessa's smile was patronizing. "Just be sure you play me straight, Detective Houston. I know how to play games. I'm rich, remember?"

Stevie sat up straight, cleared her throat in annoyance. She silently cursed her decision not to accompany the body to the morgue — at least a dead man wouldn't be giving her such attitude. "So, aren't you going to tell me why you're not falling apart over your husband's death?"

Vanessa took a lipsticked drag from her cigarette, her eyes combing Stevie and glinting with reluctant respect for Stevie's persistence. "My husband was a hedonist. He liked women, he liked to drink, he liked his food. He liked to smoke a bit of weed now and then, even snort a bit of coke — anything for a good time, you know?" She waved her cigarette in the air as she spoke. "Let's just say we weren't close friends, he and I. We've been living rather separate lives for the past ten years or so."

Stevie quirked her head, clearly puzzled. "Why did you remain married to him, then?"

Vanessa Hedley narrowed her eyes at Stevie, then blew a stream of smoke at her. "That's really none of your business, Detective."

Stevie pushed ahead. "So what you're saying is that your husband's death isn't going to be a huge loss for you?"

Vanessa glared again, then looked away.

Stevie resumed. "You were away all night?"

"Yes."

"What time did you leave the house yesterday and when did you return?"

"I left at five yesterday afternoon and returned home at about seven-thirty this morning."

Stevie recorded the terse answers in her notebook, not looking at her subject. "When did you discover your husband?"

"Right around nine."

"And when did you phone the police?"

"As soon as I saw him and felt that there was no pulse."

Stevie looked up from her task, her eyes emotionless. "Where were you all night?"

Vanessa stared unblinking, but there was a catch in her throat as she swallowed. "I refuse to answer any more questions until my lawyer is present."

CHAPTER TWO

Stevie had long ago come to expect the sickly smells associated with the morgue, but any mental preparation was always futile. Gloved and gowned, she momentarily braced herself outside the steel door, summoning all the bravado she could muster, before marching in.

The first person she saw was Tess Hewitson, who was leaning against the wall, fiercely concentrating on her shoes. She looked up when Stevie approached, a mild flicker of relief in her eyes. Obviously the young cop disliked autopsies as much as Stevie.

"Hey." Stevie smiled her sympathy. "Ready to switch professions and go into this line of work?"

Tess's smile was anemic, her face as white as a corpse. "Not on your life. I don't know how Jade does it."

Stevie shook her head. "I still haven't been able to figure that out. But if I ever do, you'll be the first to know."

She turned, looked at the body now rigid on the stainless steel table, chest wide open. Jade and a slim male assistant whom Stevie didn't recognize were both bent over it. The assistant was not much taller than Jade, and from behind, it was difficult to tell which one was which. Stevie grimaced as she watched Jade take hold of a bloody lump — the heart, Stevie guessed — and place it on a small weigh scale on the counter.

"Yuck!" Stevie exclaimed to Tess. "I hate it when they weigh the organs."

A new shade of green washed over Tess, but Stevie was too busy to notice, her eyes instead glued to Jade as she approached. Stevie smiled in spite of their surroundings.

Jade ripped off her bloody gloves, safety goggles, and mask, and shot a tired but sight-for-sore-eyes grin at Stevie. "C'mon up to my office and I can tell you what I've got. Chuck," she called over her shoulder to her assistant, "put him back together, would you?"

Stevie in turn directed the less-than-pleased Tess Hewitson to stay with the body until it was sealed back in the morgue, then followed Jade to the pale green, tiled anteroom, where Jade scrubbed her face, hands, and arms in a large, stainless steel sink.

Stevie watched, both of them comfortably silent, as

her lover of two-and-a-half years peeled off her plastic apron, then her drab green cotton scrubs. Amusement tickled Stevie at the sight of Jade's boxer shorts, which were emblazoned with the Metropolitan Toronto Police insignia — a gift from Stevie. It was something much more intense than amusement, however, that tickled Stevie's insides as her eyes glided over Jade's compact legs, flat stomach, small but still firm breasts sheathed in a sports bra, and that smooth, oh-so-kissable neck. Stevie watched Jade slip on fresh scrubs — she knew Jade wouldn't put on her street clothes until she'd had a long, cleansing shower. But the thought of Jade in her boyishly baggy, hip-hugging, faded jeans and loose oversize shirt made Stevie grin and long for their evening at home.

Jade looked at Stevie. "Don't you look like the cat that swallowed the canary."

Stevie's grin grew as wide as Lake Ontario, her wink slow like the setting sun. "Just making plans for tonight, that's all."

Jade pushed the door to the corridor open, holding it for Stevie. "Well, don't make too many. I'll probably be asleep by the time you feed me dinner and a glass of wine."

Stevie punched the up button outside the elevator, her voice dropping to a whisper. "No problem. But don't tell me you're not up to a good massage."

Jade sighed her approval, love lighting up her eyes, then dimming as concentration etched its way onto her forehead. She glanced at the wrinkled papers in her hand. It was time to talk business, and, taking the cue, Stevie began filling her in on what she knew of the case so far.

Jade slouched in the chair behind her desk and

hoisted her tired feet up. She sighed heavily. "This is the first I think I've sat down in about seven hours. It feels more like seven days."

"I wish there was something I could do to help you, so long as it didn't entail doing anything in the morgue."

"Don't worry, there's plenty of work to go around for you, too. I doubt you'll be home much before eight tonight yourself."

Stevie nodded drearily. "I'll give Paul and Rick a call and ask them if they can feed Tonka and let her out."

Jade sighed at the mention of their eighteen-month-old golden retriever. "Poor dog. Thank God for Paul and Rick. Knowing them, they'll probably just keep her until we get home. *And* overfeed her."

"Who's your new assistant, by the way?"

Jade waved a dismissive hand. "Oh, Chuck O'Leary. He was hired a couple of months ago on a contract to fill in for Kathleen while she's on her pregnancy leave. Seems competent enough but sure doesn't talk much."

"So what have you found?"

Jade flattened the sheets of paper she'd brought up from the morgue, her own words and sketches hastily penciled on them. "Did I tell you the damn mike broke three autopsies ago? Couldn't record a damn thing."

Stevie frowned. "That's great."

"Another reason why I can't wait for this day to end. Had to write everything out by hand. Anyway," she sighed loudly. "I'd say heroin did the deed, but there may have been coke as well. We'll have to wait a few days for the toxicology results. And you guys were right about just one fresh needle mark. No history there of needle use that I can see."

"How can you be so sure about the heroin at this point?" Stevie asked, her notebook open, pen poised.

Jade pulled her feet off the desk and sat up, elbows on the desktop, her voice invigorated. "All the signs are there: fluid in the lungs and froth in the windpipe, his mouth, and nose. In a heroin overdose, everything slows down and the person basically forgets to breathe and goes into a coma. Then they essentially drown from all the fluid seeping out of the blood vessels."

"What does coke do?"

"Much faster. It sends weird electric impulses to the heart, causing arrhythmia, and it kills pretty quickly. With heroin, it can take a couple of hours. Did you guys find any coke lying around the house?"

Stevie wrote quickly while she answered. "Don't know yet. They're still going through the place. But it looked like a pretty big party, and we both know coke is no stranger to Rosedale parties."

"You got that right," Jade agreed. "I don't how some of those people can do that shit and hold on to their hundred-grand-a-year jobs. Anyway, I scraped the inside of Mr. Hedley's nose to see."

Stevie underlined something in her notebook. "I think time of death is going to make or break our case against Mrs. Hedley. She says she noticed her husband dead at around nine this morning." Stevie, always the cynic, made a face. "Her story is that she was out all night and got home at about seven-thirty."

Jade nodded somewhat indifferently. Her job was to provide Stevie with clues from the most important piece of evidence — the body. It was up to Stevie to take those clues and make something of them. Jade always took an interest in how Stevie solved her cases, but right now, her focus was on the body she'd just autopsied. "So you need to know if she could have injected him in those ninety minutes."

"Exactly."

Jade pushed her worn leather chair back — everything in her tiny office was second hand — and went to the coffee maker on a table near the window. She spooned unmeasured coffee grounds into a fresh filter and poured a practiced amount of water from a bottle of nearby Evian.

"There's a lot of lividity on his underside, and when I checked it almost two hours ago now, the skin still blanched." They both glanced at the wall clock, which read three minutes after two, as Jade returned to her chair. "So that would put time of death at six to eight hours before. Rigor's consistent with that too."

Stevie did the mental math and scratched in her notebook: *Time of death, approx. 4 to 6 a.m.* "Does body temp support that too?"

Jade's smile was full of admiration for Stevie, who was almost always a step ahead. She glanced at her stained notes. "Don't worry, I'm getting to that. When I began the autopsy it was ninety-four point five. Did Benton take it at the scene?"

Stevie shook her head.

Jade's full lips pursed in suppressed frustration. "Damn, I should have gone to the scene. What was the temperature in the bedroom?"

Stevie hurriedly flipped through her notebook. "I noticed the thermostat at seventy-five degrees. It was pretty warm."

"All right, you'll need to ask the wife if she touched the thermostat. The room's temperature will affect my calculations."

Stevie nodded.

"The bad news is, body temperature isn't going to help us much in this case. A body typically cools one degree every hour after death."

Another mental calculation from Stevie. "That would put his death at, what, eight this morning?"

"Right," Jade nodded. "And while that puts the wife there at the scene, rigor, algor, and lividity don't support death occurring that late. And don't forgot, heroin doesn't usually kill very quickly — coma happens first."

Stevie nodded again as she wrote in her notebook. If Vanessa Hedley was the killer, she couldn't have injected her husband between seven-thirty and nine A.M. The fatal dose had been given much earlier. Still, Stevie was somewhat confused about the conflicting facts.

"So you're saying the body didn't cool down much because of the high temperature in the room?" Stevie asked.

"Yes, that and the fact that Mr. Hedley was overweight. And if he'd been doing coke at this party, that heightens body temperature."

The coffee maker had quieted, and Stevie stood up to do the honors.

"About the needle mark, Jade. It —"

Fire alarms from the hallway shrilled; Stevie and Jade exchanged annoyed glances.

"Shit," Jade swore as they hurried down the stairs with the rest of the staff. "I really did not need this today."

They stood outside the brown brick Ontario Coroner's Office with the dozens of other employees, watching fire trucks block Grosvenor Street, firefighters spilling from the big, pale green machines.

Jade paced away her irritation. "Christ, I hope this doesn't go on long."

"Probably just an alarm," Stevie shrugged. What she really wanted was to take Jade in her arms and give her a huge hug. "I'm sure it won't be long. There's no sign of any smoke or anything." She, too, was growing anxious to get back to work.

Jade brushed a hand through dark, boyishly short hair, her dark green eyes scanning the crowd. "Shit, where the hell is Chuck?"

"Your assistant?" Stevie asked.

"I know he would have heard the alarms if he was still down in the morgue. The place is wired up like a minefield. I just hope he's all right."

Stevie spotted Tess Hewitson chatting with a firefighter and waved her over.

Stevie put her arm around the broad shoulders of the young officer. "What's going on, Tess?"

"I was just coming out when the alarms went off. I was about to head back to my division."

"So the postmortem was done?" Jade asked her pointedly.

Tess nodded. "We'd finished up a couple of minutes before. 'Course, I couldn't get out of there fast enough."

"What about Chuck O'Leary?" Jade pressed worriedly. "We haven't seen him come out."

Tess surveyed the crowd of workers and onlookers and shrugged. "Last I saw, he was cleaning up. But he might be hanging around helping the firefighters down there. One of them just told me it was a garbage can fire somewhere in the basement."

Jade exhaled loudly, her shoulders relaxing. "Good. I'm glad it's nothing serious."

Word began drifting through the crowd that the all-clear had been given. Stevie and Jade said their good-byes to Tess, with Stevie promising to get together soon, and joined the parade back into the building. None seemed as eager as Stevie and Jade to get back to work.

"About that needle mark on Hedley's arm," Stevie said, continuing their earlier conversation. "I want to be ready for some of the questions any defense lawyer worth their salt is going to ask."

Jade nodded and headed toward the stairs, the wait too long for the elevator. "Yes, I know what you're going to ask, and it would be very tricky for Hedley to have injected himself in that area of his right arm. And from my examination of his hands, and his watch being on his left wrist, he doesn't look to be left-handed."

"Any hesitation marks?"

"Clean as a whistle. No problem finding the vein. And with Hedley not being a regular needle user, it doesn't look like the mark of a novice." She glanced at Stevie over her shoulder. "Trust me, you'd have to be pretty good at it to give yourself an injection with your off hand."

Stevie followed Jade up the stairs, enjoying the view. "Did I tell you Vanessa Hedley attended medical school for a couple of years?"

Jade halted so suddenly that Stevie nearly crashed into her.

"Chuck!" Jade exclaimed at the thin, balding,

thirty-something man two steps above her. "Where have you been?" she asked him in a voice that could peel paint. "Did you not hear the alarms?"

He tried to smile, but seemed too nervous to manage anything more than a grimace. He couldn't look at them, his eyes darting from the walls to the stairs. "I did, but I thought I could put the fire out by myself."

"The garbage can fire?" Jade asked.

He nodded, the Adam's apple bobbing frantically in his scrawny throat, as if it were doing all the talking. "It was my fault, I take full responsibility, and I promise it won't happen again."

"What happened?"

"After the PM, after I'd finished cleaning up and everything, I . . ." he glanced up at the ceiling, buying time, then at his hands, which he began wringing. "I had a smoke and threw the butt in the garbage can, and it caught."

Jade shook her head slowly, and Stevie knew she was biting back harsh words — or maybe saving them for later. "You're right. It won't happen again. Now isn't there some work you could be doing, rather than roaming the building?"

"I, actually, I was looking for you so I could explain what happened." He gestured in an exaggerated way like a child would.

Jade's eyes left him, her cue that their little meeting was over, and she continued up the stairs. Stevie knew that people often underestimated Jade. Her beauty and her habit of observing the action, rather than being at the center of it, gave the false impression that she was a lightweight. Stevie smiled.

Her lover was anything but, and Chuck O'Leary had probably just learned it the hard way.

"One more thing about Hedley," Jade added as they finally reached her floor. "He had about seven hundred cubic centimeters of urine in his bladder."

Always the butch, Stevie pushed Jade's office door open and stood aside to let her pass. "And that means what?"

"He hadn't urinated in hours, and that much urine in your bladder would leave you very uncomfortable. Again, it means he'd been dead or in a coma for several hours. Ah, shit!" Jade shrieked, scurrying to her desk. "Goddamn sprinklers were triggered."

Jade cursed again, and Stevie spotted the cause of this latest irritation. The papers on her desk, including her rough autopsy notes on James Hedley, were soaked — ruined.

"Shit," Stevie agreed solemnly. She knew what this would mean to any defense lawyer. No tape and now no original notes from the postmortem. All Jade had to go on was her memory.

They would have to hope it was enough for a jury some day.

CHAPTER THREE

Stevie returned to the Roxborough neighborhood to give her partner a hand with the monotonous legwork. The faster they could talk to neighbors of the Hedleys, the fresher the night's events would be in their minds.

Stevie had put off telling Jovanowski about the ruined autopsy notes — she'd tell him eventually. There was no sense in adding to his sour mood.

They worked through dinner hour, dividing up the houses in the immediate neighborhood to find out who'd seen what. The neighbors had all noticed a big party at the Hedleys's the night before, beginning at about nine P.M. and ending at about three or four A.M. Nothing remarkable, just the usual party noise and drunks stumbling down the driveway to waiting taxis, or worse, to their own cars.

There was one more house, directly behind the Hedleys's, and the two detectives decided to tackle that one together. Wearily, they trudged up the interlocking brick walkway.

An elderly woman, her hair perfectly coiffed, her chiffon dress perfectly unwrinkled, answered the bright red door of the Victorian-style house. Stevie and Jovanowski introduced themselves, explained in vague terms what had happened to James Hedley, and told her they needed to know if she'd seen or heard anything unusual in the neighborhood during the early morning hours.

The woman's heeled leather shoes clicked on Italian ceramic as she led them into what decades ago would have been called the parlor, a high-ceilinged room with shiny hardwood floors, oak trim, and a marble fireplace.

Stevie and Jovanowski sat down on the floral love seat offered to them.

"May I get you a cup of tea, or coffee perhaps?" the woman, who'd identified herself as Mrs. Beatrice Robinson, asked in a formal but welcome tone.

Both detectives, anxious to call it a day, politely declined the offer. It was after seven, and the faint smell of a slow-cooking roast teased their empty stomachs.

"This shouldn't take long," Stevie assured the woman.

Beatrice Robinson floated into a matching floral wing chair, crossed her silk-stockinged legs, and sat straight as a board, hands lightly clasped in her lap like a choirgirl. She reminded Stevie of how her own mother would probably act in a situation like this, where all the manners and behavior codes of a well-bred, well-moneyed life ruled above all else. No matter what the horror of the situation, decorum was everything.

Stevie unwillingly found herself remembering her twin sister Sarah's funeral, and how her mother's poise never wavered. She'd even scolded five-year-old Stevie for wailing in public. Repressed emotions were the only emotions allowed in the Houston home.

Stevie felt the prick of decades-old anger toward her mother and swallowed hard. It pissed her off that her family could still hammer her emotionally, even though she'd effectively written them off years ago.

"Mrs. Robinson, what time did you go to bed last night?" Jovanowski was asking, much less gruffly than he usually asked questions, particularly at the end of a day.

"It was at eleven-thirty, just as soon as the news was over."

"What about your husband?" Jovanowski continued.

"I'm a widow, Detective Jovanowski."

Jovanowski cleared his throat and mumbled an apology. "Had you noticed before then anything unusual at the Hedley residence?"

"Well, there seemed to be a party going on," she offered, speaking slowly and clearly, sure of every word. The perfect witness. "There were cars and people coming and going, some noise. But nothing extremely loud. You see, from my bedroom window, I have a good view of their driveway."

Stevie wrote in her notebook. "Were there often parties at the Hedleys's?"

"Oh yes, probably about once a month. But nothing to call the police about." She smiled slightly. "You can be certain I would place a call to the police if things were to get too undesirable."

"And so you went to bed at about eleven-thirty," Stevie continued. "Did you sleep the rest of the night?"

Another smile. "My dear, when you get to be my age, believe me, the old bladder isn't what it used to be."

Stevie smiled back, liking this woman in spite of her affluent texture and all the distasteful things Stevie associated with it.

"I got up at about four and was just curious as to whether things had died down over there, so I looked out the bedroom window." She had begun twirling her pearl necklace with smooth fingers.

"And?" Jovanowski prompted.

"I saw a blond woman walking quickly down the driveway, toward the road. I'm quite sure it was Vanessa Hedley, because I remember wondering where she was going at that time of night, and that perhaps they'd had another fight or something —"

"Another fight?" Stevie interrupted. "Did they fight a lot?"

Mrs. Robinson shook her head lightly in silent admonishment. It was clear she didn't believe in public displays of disagreements. "I'm afraid they had some horrendous yelling matches, at least once or twice a month."

Jovanowski led her back to the previous night's events. "So you're not sure it was Mrs. Hedley you saw early this morning?"

The twisting of her necklace continued as she squinted in concentration. "No, I really can't, Detective. I only saw her from the back. I just assumed it was her was because she had short blond hair and was fairly thin."

Stevie felt relief. A witness who wanted to help, but wasn't about to embellish or say she was sure of something when she really wasn't. Overzealous witnesses were a pain in the ass, Stevie knew from experience.

"What was she wearing?" Stevie asked.

The woman shrugged delicately. "It was dark. I could tell it was a dress . . . a dark dress, but that's it, I'm afraid."

"Did you see this woman go to a car, or a taxi?" Jovanowski asked.

Mrs. Robinson shook her head. "I couldn't see that far down the driveway. I really don't know where she went, but she looked full of . . ." She quirked her head ever so slightly, searching for the right phrase. "Full of purpose, that's it."

"Like, in a hurry?" Stevie suggested.

Mrs. Robinson considered for a moment, and finally agreed. "Yes, she was not running."

"Do you remember anything else about last night?" Stevie prompted.

Mrs. Robinson shook her head regretfully, as

though she wished she had more to give them. "I'm afraid that's all I saw."

Stevie and Jovanowski stood in unison. It was Jovanowski who spoke. "We'll be in touch, Mrs. Robinson. I'm sure we'll have more questions again some time."

The chardonnay was chilling in the fridge, the dijon sauce simmering on the range, the chicken sputtering to crispy perfection in the oven. Even the dog lay contented as Stevie uncharacteristically puttered in the kitchen, waiting for Jade. She glanced impatiently at the wall clock again, listening for Jade's key in the front door lock.

Finally, Stevie balled up her apron and tossed it on the counter. To hell with it, she'd open the wine. Pulling the cork, Stevie poured herself a glass and took a healthy sip. The phone rang just as she was setting her glass down on the counter.

It was Jade.

"Are you on your way home or what?" Stevie asked, knowing she was sounding horribly grumpy.

"Sorry, hon, not yet. It's the damnedest thing," Jade said breathlessly. "Vanessa Hedley came in a little while ago to collect her husband's things. Jesus, I still can't believe it!"

Stevie bristled at the mention of Vanessa Hedley, a woman she'd taken an instant disliking to. "Believe what?"

"It's Vanessa," Jade practically shouted. "Can you believe it?"

"What are you talking about?"

"My old friend from med school, Vanessa Smith. I didn't even know she lived in Toronto, or what her married name was, and . . ."

Stevie listened to Jade rattle on about her long-lost friend, until it dawned on her. She was incredulous, though not in the obviously amused way that Jade was.

"Wait a minute, Jade. Are you saying this is the same Vanessa that you were lovers with back in college?"

"Yes, of course. Anyway, she's quite upset about what's happened and —"

"Oh she is, is she? Funny, she wasn't too upset earlier."

Jade ignored Stevie's cutting remark. "She's asked me to go out for dinner and a drink with her, so I don't know when I'll be back."

"Jade," Stevie cautioned, "you really should be careful. She's the primary subject of our investigation right now, and with you having done the post-mortem —"

"I know, I know. You don't have to play cop with me, Stevie." Jade's irritation was coming through loud and clear. "Don't worry, I'll be careful. I won't discuss anything about the case with her."

Stevie felt uneasy as she put down the phone and took a long gulp of wine. She wasn't sure if the sinking feeling in her stomach was from an ex-lover walking back into Jade's life or from a murder suspect worming into her and Jade's inner sanctum. Whatever it was, it wasn't welcome. And the fact that her romantic dinner plans were down the tube made her mad as hell.

Tonka barked at the ringing doorbell, startling Stevie from her brooding.

"Hey, Tess," Stevie smiled wanly at her friend. "There goes the neighborhood."

"I was out for a walk and thought I'd stop in for a minute." Her smile was three feet wide, the freckles on her face finally absorbed by her tan. It had taken the blond all summer to discard her various shades of pink. "Hi, girl." She patted Tonka, who sat in eager readiness for all the attention she could get.

"C'mon in. You can rescue me from a lonely, burned dinner."

Tess followed Stevie to the kitchen. "Where's Jade?"

"Don't ask," Stevie mumbled, reaching for a wineglass for Tess.

"I've already eaten, but thanks for the offer."

Stevie poured her friend a glass, smirking. "What'd you have for dinner? And don't bullshit me, because I remember what single people eat for dinner. Was it McDonald's or a TV dinner?"

Tess grinned and accepted the glass of chardonnay. "All right, I confess. It was a Wendy's spicy chicken sandwich."

Stevie laughed, momentarily forgetting her dark mood. "Then you're having some of my home cooking. And you'd better take me up on the offer, because it's a rare thing, you know. Jade's the cook around here."

"Hmm, then, I don't know . . ." Tess teased. She didn't relent until Stevie gave her a good butch-to-butch wallop on the arm.

They ate dinner, Stevie less heartily than Tess, and avoided work in conversation. They talked about women's hockey, about Tess's ice-cold love life, gossiped about people they both knew.

Later, while still sipping wine, Tess pulled from her shirt pocket a couple of cigars from a silver tube. "Is Jade going to kill us if she smells cigars when she comes home?" She winked conspiratorially.

Stevie laughed and gratefully took one of the cigars: a dark brown, thick Nicaraguan. "If these taste as good as they smell, it'll be worth whatever hell there is to pay."

Tess had introduced Stevie to the art of smoking fine cigars, and it was something Stevie liked to do a couple of times a week in spite of Jade's protestations.

"So," said Tess haltingly as they each drew on their cigars. "Who burned your toast today?"

Stevie winced, inhaled again, held it, then blew out a mouthful of smoke. "Sorry I'm in an ugly. It's just this case I'm working on." She didn't feel like discussing Jade's latest revelation about Vanessa Hedley being her ex-lover. And Stevie was grudgingly beginning to admit to herself it was their history together, and not the fact that Vanessa was the main murder suspect in her case, that had her blood boiling.

Tess leaned forward, the cigar nestled between her fingers, her ice blue eyes kindling with excitement. "So tell me what you've got so far?"

Stevie shook her head lightly, a smile tugging at the corners of her mouth. Tess was so much like a younger version of herself.

Stevie filled her in on what little she knew, sprinkled with her own observations and gut feelings. Homicide investigation was methodical, a real science, and it could all be learned. But experience and instinct were things that could not be learned or shortcutted, Stevie knew. And in spite of Tess's keenness, her goal of joining Stevie on the homicide squad would take time and nurturing, and a fine teacher. Stevie smiled as she exhaled smoke and thought of how proud it would make her to have a protégé make the elite squad.

CHAPTER FOUR

Stevie felt the scowl sweeping across her face like a black curtain. She leaned her back into the wall, arms crossed over her chest, and stared with ill-disguised contempt at the seated Vanessa Hedley. Jovanowski was outside the conference room going over the ground rules of the interview with Vanessa's lawyer, so it was just Stevie and the rich bitch, locked in an agreement of silence that felt more like a demilitarized zone than a peace treaty.

Stevie resented Vanessa for having spent more of

the weekend with Jade than she had; begrudged bitterly the fact that, even though it had been years ago, Vanessa, too, had tasted Jade, had felt Jade's hands all over her, her lips . . . Stevie's chest felt suddenly heavy, like an Earth Mover was tromping over it. Her imagination played out visions she really didn't want to see. Could Vanessa possibly guess that Stevie was now the recipient of those lips, the subject of those masterful hands?

Get a grip, Houston, she told herself. *If you can't, you'd better get your ass off this case.*

The door opened suddenly. Jovanowski motioned for everyone to sit at the long table worn glassy smooth by thousands of meetings such as this one.

"Stevie, this is Laura Redgrave." He jerked his head toward the tall, thin, middle-aged woman whose dark blue power suit and curt movements suggested she was all business. Today, Stevie wore her own power suit: forest green dress pants crisply starched and pressed, black collarless shirt and black blazer jacket, her pistol enveloped within the folds. She could play this game too.

Like a warrior preparing for battle, Vanessa's lawyer removed a thick, leather covered binder from her briefcase and set it on the table in front of her like a shield. Then she pulled out a bulky *1998 Criminal Code* — her club — and thumped it on the table.

"Detectives," she cleared her throat and continued in a low, even voice, "I'd like you to show me in this *Criminal Code* exactly what charge you are laying against my client."

Stevie and Jovanowski, seated shoulder to shoulder

across from lawyer and client, shot each other an exasperated glance. They knew they had diddly on their main suspect, knew this lawyer knew it too.

"Your client," Stevie acknowledged, "is not facing any charges at the moment. We are simply on a fact-finding mission."

Redgrave shot up, her chair scraping the polished floor, her dark eyes like little cannonballs. "Then we have nothing further to discuss until which time my client has been charged."

Quietly, Vanessa tugged at her lawyer's expensive sleeve and they whispered for a moment before Redgrave sat down again. She tapped a gold-plated pen impatiently on her leather binder.

Stevie couldn't help but feel that it was all a big show, rehearsed and nailed on the first take. It was a ploy to make Vanessa Hedley look like she really did want to cooperate, that it was her lawyer preventing her from doing so.

"Detectives, my client is interested in what information you are seeking from her, and would like to see her husband's murder solved." Redgrave looked, slit-eyed, at both Stevie and Jovanowski. "But I must caution you that we will choose which questions, if any, we wish to answer. I also want to know what so-called evidence you might have against my client."

The two detectives nodded, and Stevie switched on a tape recorder. Both sides had their own tape recorders and would make their own written notes.

They went through Vanessa's actions from the time she had walked into her home two days ago to the discovery of her husband's body and her call to police. She hadn't touched anything, she said, hadn't noticed anything missing or vandalized in the house. At least she wasn't being the smart ass she had been earlier when Stevie interviewed her, Stevie thought with amusement and with a small sense of victory. Perhaps the seriousness of the detectives' interest in her had scared her a little.

They talked about James Hedley's recreational drug use, his affinity to parties and promiscuity, the conversation devoid of emotion. Though Vanessa readily admitted the marriage had been over for years and that she had never really loved James Hedley, her coolness still struck Stevie as odd.

Not many people had liked her husband, Vanessa added. He was cold, devious, self-absorbed and used people. All that really mattered to him were money and social status.

Didn't seem to be just James Hedley those things mattered to, Stevie thought bitterly. *God, what did Jade ever see in her?*

"Who did your husband hang out with? Who would he have partied with?" Stevie asked.

Vanessa shrugged, looking genuine for once. "I think a few of them were his coworkers. I'm not exactly sure." She frowned. "Like I said, we lived under the same roof, but that was about it."

Jovanowski asked, "Did your husband ever abuse you or threaten you in any way, Mrs. Hedley?"

Vanessa shook her head unequivocally. Stevie wanted to ask why she would stay in such a marriage, knew Jovanowski was wondering the same thing. Did she use drugs? Stevie asked. No. As a former medical school student, did she know much about cocaine and heroin and their effects? Vanessa refused to answer. Did the open marriage apply to her also? Another refusal.

Stevie set her pen down and snapped her notebook shut, knowing she wouldn't need either with her next question. She stared at Vanessa for a long moment, her dark brown eyes desperately struggling to mask the jealousy she felt and hated. She set her jaw in this inner battle with her unprofessional feelings. She took a deep, slow breath. "Where were you last Friday night, the ninth of September?"

Vanessa glanced at her lawyer, waited for her to bail her out. Predictably, her safety ring arrived.

"That is not a question we are prepared to answer at this time, and in fact will not answer until you have enough evidence for a preliminary trial," Laura Redgrave answered forcefully.

Stevie smirked, her eyes glinting. "What are you hiding, Vanessa?" It was almost a whisper and unmistakably accusatory. "Who are you protecting?"

For an instant, Vanessa's blue eyes flared in surprise and her hands twitched as though she would give anything for a cigarette at this moment. Stevie smiled her satisfaction.

Redgrave leapt up from her chair, pointing at Stevie to punctuate her outrage. "You are badgering my client, Detective Houston. It is uncalled for and, if it persists, this interview is over." She sat back down, slowly, as though she begrudged any further discussion.

Stevie simply nodded. Her point had been made.

The lawyer cleared her throat. "What evidence do you have against my client, detectives?"

It was Jovanowski's turn to take over. He would tell the lawyer what they had against Vanessa Hedley so far, show that they had begun building a case against her. The detectives had nothing to be coy about, no trump card up their sleeves. Just old-fashioned police work.

"Vanessa Hedley has no alibi for the night of the murder." He spoke in a measured tone, as if reading from a prepared text. "She was in an unhappy marriage and stood to inherit a life insurance policy of half a million dollars upon her husband's death, plus the house, investments, and whatever else belonged to James Hedley."

"How do you know that?" the lawyer barked.

Jovanowski pulled a piece of paper from the file folder in front of him. "I have a warrant right here. We seized a copy of the will today."

Redgrave snatched the paper from Jovanowski's hand and skimmed it.

"I'd say your client is a *very* rich woman now, Ms. Redgrave." Jovanowski's benign smile contrasted the razor sharpness of his words.

"What else?" the lawyer asked in a bored manner as she handed the warrant back.

"Your client has the knowledge to commit this crime, being a former medical student —"

"She dropped out before finishing," Redgrave cut in.

Jovanowski ignored her. "Mrs. Hedley had full access to the house, obviously. We also have a witness who places your client at the house at a time when your client says she wasn't there."

Vanessa whispered hurriedly to her lawyer.

"That's impossible," Redgrave said casually. "Who's your witness?"

Stevie jumped in. "We're not at liberty to reveal

that just yet. But perhaps," she looked at Vanessa, "if your client can reveal her whereabouts on the night in question, our witness will be irrelevant."

The lawyer sniffed. "So in other words you don't have a strong witness. And we will not answer as to Mrs. Hedley's whereabouts at this time."

Stevie caught Jovanowski's sideways glance. She had to give Redgrave credit. The woman had balls.

"Is that it, then?" Redgrave asked, then stood. Her left hand absently flicked her auburn hair from her shoulder. "Because if it is, detectives, I'd say you've got shit."

Stevie switched the tape recorder off, wanting to smile at the lawyer's choice of words. Redgrave was right, of course. All they had was circumstantial evidence that would never hold up in court. They needed something else — a solid witness, the syringe with Vanessa's prints on it, something. Without those, the chances of convicting Vanessa Hedley without a confession were slim to none. The house and grounds had already been thoroughly searched, the neighborhood canvassed for further witnesses, all to no avail. Tomorrow they'd begin interviewing people who knew James Hedley, including partygoers.

After the duo left, Jovanowski plunked himself on the corner of the conference table, shaking his head in resignation. "That sure didn't get us very far."

Stevie hoisted her feet up on the chair beside her, feeling more cocky than her partner. "Yeah, but if Vanessa thinks we're concentrating everything on her it might make her sweat a little."

Jovanowski disagreed. "Not enough for a confession. She's a pretty cool customer."

"Which is exactly why she very well could have committed this murder, Ted."

Jovanowski shook his head again. "You heard her, though. It sounds like her husband was hated. Hell, it could even have been some jealous broad he was screwing, or his coke connection offing him for being behind on his payments. And you can bet that Redgrave bitch would drag every last scenario into the courtroom."

Stevie nodded as she chewed the cap of her Bic. "Ted, if we can find out where Vanessa was that night and what she was doing, I think we'll have a hell of a lot of answers."

Stevie was restless. Walking the dog for two miles, while a treat for Tonka, did nothing to ease her tension. She was not happy that it was nine in the evening and Jade was still not home. A hasty note had simply said Vanessa had had a rough day and needed a friend.

What about me, Stevie wanted to scream. *Maybe I had a rough day too.*

It was more than just her irritation with Jade lately. Vanessa was occupying Stevie's thoughts almost every minute. This wasn't unusual, Stevie reassured herself. All good detectives got a little obsessed with their suspects; it was the only way they could really get inside their heads. But Stevie couldn't separate the professional obsessing from her own jealousy, and she hated it. It made her feel so adolescent, so unprofessional.

Stevie poured herself a glass of bourbon, absently stroked Tonka's golden head, and stared at nothing for a long while. When she suddenly jumped out of her chair, it startled Tonka into a barking frenzy.

"Shh, it's okay, girl."

Somewhere, Jade had an old yearbook from medical school. Stevie remembered seeing it among Jade's boxes of books when they'd moved in together two years ago. If she could just find it, maybe there was something in it about Vanessa. What that was, Stevie had no idea. Or even why she had to find those books. *Obsessing again.*

She ran up the stairs and first browsed the shelves of books in their joint office. Nothing. Then the shelves on either side of the fireplace in the living room. Still nothing. Lastly, Stevie went to their bedroom, Tonka obediently behind her. Books spilled from the shelving units, but no medical school yearbooks.

Stevie opened the large double closet doors. On top of the shelf hovering over the racks of clothes were three dusty boxes. On a mission now, Stevie carefully pulled the boxes down and set them on the floor. She tried to ignore the momentary twinge of guilt for going through boxes that weren't hers. Staring at them, hands on her hips, she reasoned that the boxes were in their joint closet, after all. And besides, she and Jade had no secrets from each other. So what the hell.

The first box contained binders of yellowed notes from some long ago university classes of Jade's. There were notes on physics, human anatomy, biochemistry — stuff that was completely foreign to Stevie. They might as well have been written in Chinese for all Stevie could decipher of them. The next box contained a couple of warped textbooks, a dusty framed photo of Jade in a wedding dress — Stevie smiled at that — an old high school report card (all *As*), an Emily Dickinson book of poetry, and a couple of letters from Jade's mother, one dated 1982 and one 1983. Stevie didn't read them.

The contents of the third box looked much like that of the first two — more papers and books. Stevie wondered why Jade was keeping most of it. She dug to the bottom, felt two thin, hardcover books, and pulled them to the surface. *Bull's-eye!* "University of Toronto School of Medicine," Stevie read aloud. One was dated Class of 1985, the other Class of 1984.

Stevie sat down on the plush carpet and raced through the more recent book. Quickly, she found Jade's grad photo, but no Vanessa Smith. Dummy, she muttered to herself, remembering that Vanessa hadn't finished med school. She grabbed the second book and looked up the third years, thumbed the pages until she found Vanessa's photo.

Stevie stared glumly at a young, vivacious, and gorgeous Vanessa Smith. Smile wide and innocent, eyes hopeful and a touch mischievous. *Too damned good looking.* Below the photo were a few words. *Goal: To finish school and make lots of money as a surgeon. Favorite phrase: Eat my dust. Best buddy: Jade Agawa-Garneau.*

Stevie seethed at the last words, suddenly craving the drink she'd left downstairs. It had been Vanessa's final full year at school, Jade had told Stevie. At the beginning of the third year, Vanessa had promptly announced, to even Jade's surprise, that she was getting married and dropping out of school. Jade hadn't seen her again, until now.

Jade had never mentioned Vanessa's name to Stevie in the two and a half years they'd been together. She had only casually mentioned that her first female relationship took place in university. Both she and her girlfriend eventually decided to marry men, she'd told Stevie. All very matter of fact. Stevie hadn't pressed Jade for further details, assuming the relationship with Vanessa had been a fairly shallow, transient one.

Stevie was flipping through the book again, hoping for another glimpse of Vanessa or Jade, when three pieces of paper dropped onto her lap, each still crisp and neatly folded. Tossing the book aside, Stevie snapped up the first paper. At the top was the date March 1, 1984. *To My Wonderful Sweet Jade*, it began. Jumping to the bottom, Stevie looked to see who it was from: *Lovingly, Your Dearest Vanessa.*

Stevie winced in repulsion, felt the urge to gag. But her flippancy soon dissolved as she read:

> *I've been thinking about you all day. Well, mostly I've been thinking about your lips, and your tongue, and the way they tasted after they made me come. God, Jade, I wish you could live down there. You have no idea how good you are, or what a sweet piece you are, my darling! I can't stop thinking about your cunt too, and the way it tastes and the way it wants me so much. I had you begging last night, remember? With you in my bed, I could never* (will never) *want anyone else. With you I am complete, and I only hope I can make you half as happy as you've made me these last few weeks. I want to*

marry you some day (and I mean that with all my heart!)

Lovingly,

Your Dearest Vanessa

P.S. Sweet dreams, my love. I'm sorry we can't be together tonight, but I'll see you tomorrow.

Stevie's unblinking eyes were riveted on the words, as though they might leap off the page in all their ugliness. She agonizingly repeated them in her mind, the sex words driving a stake into her gut, piercing her jealousy, taunting the green-eyed monster within. She knew in her head that it was silly, but the words made her feel like Jade was somehow being unfaithful to her, that it was all still fresh. It hurt like hell — that much was fresh. *Damn Jade for keeping this stupid letter!*

Again Stevie read the letter until she felt like she owned the words, until she'd dulled their bite. Far more disturbing to Stevie, once she'd calmed down, was the gradual dawning that there had been nothing casual about this past relationship of Jade's.

Stevie picked up the second note much less eagerly than she had picked up the first. It was dated just three months after the love letter.

Jade:

I'm sorry, but we cannot see each other ever again, at least not in the way we have. There is nothing to explain. We just got carried away in our friendship, and it is now time for each of us to move on. Please don't tell anyone about us.

Vanessa

Stevie felt the shock of the harsh words. *That bitch!* She'd shed Jade like a bad cold. How could Jade possibly be giving her the time of day now, after what Vanessa had done to her? Stevie was dumbfounded.

She flipped to the third letter, this one from Jade to Vanessa, and dated a week after the Dear John letter. Obviously Jade had never bothered to send the letter.

Vanessa:

I guess you really are serious about not wanting to see me, since you won't even take my calls. I haven't decided whether or not to send this, since you would probably just rip it up without reading it. How could you do this to me, Vanessa, to us? I thought we loved each other. At least I thought you loved me, and I know I DESPERATELY love you! I wanted us to spend the rest of our lives together!!! We had so many wonderful times together, it was magical, I thought. And now all of a sudden this. I don't understand, Vanessa. I don't understand you, and I guess I no longer understand what we had. Please explain things to me. Please, I wish you wanted me again like those times when I could drive you crazy just by looking at you. What's happened?????? You have no idea how much you've hurt me, Vanessa.

Waiting,
Jade

Stevie shoved the boxes back in the closet but saved the three letters for her pocket. She needed that damn drink. Needed ten drinks. Maybe, she hoped, the booze would dull the realization that this thing between Jade and Vanessa had been far more complicated, much more fathomless, than she had feared.

Jade knew — had known from the start — that Vanessa was holding something back. In their days together all those years ago, she had always been frustratingly reticent, never able to truly give one hundred per cent of herself to anyone. Jade had realized that too late.

When she first found out that the murdered James Hedley was Vanessa's husband, Jade's curiosity took over. For a time, she had known Vanessa like no one else. She'd briefly cracked that cement exterior, had seen the neediness there, had felt Vanessa's yearning to be loved and accepted. It had been a special time, Jade's first love affair with a woman, and she would cherish that time always. It had been exciting, like driving her first car. Neat in a nostalgic way. The way her first beat-up old Volkswagen had been. But that was then. Stevie was her Cadillac now.

Jade had long ago forgiven Vanessa for the callous breakup. In retrospect, she couldn't be happier, because she knew real love now. Thanks to Vanessa, she had something to compare it too.

Jade was curious about the Vanessa of today, with whom she had sat sipping tea in her hotel room. Was she a murderer, this woman she'd once cared so much for? The investigator in her would not rest until she found out, Jade knew. And she would help Stevie, would go where a stranger with a badge couldn't, her bond with Vanessa her conduit.

Jade and Vanessa had spent a lot of time together since the murder, some of it in silence, some of it strolling down memory lane. Vanessa had seemed all too happy to have Jade drop everything for her, just like in the old days. Perhaps she was using Jade now, perhaps not. But Jade could be cunning too. Jade had her own agenda.

Jade broke the silence. "Why did you stay with him all these years, Vanessa? Was it the money?"

Vanessa refilled her teacup, her eyes focused on her task. "Partly, I guess. And partly because I didn't need to leave." She dragged her eyes to Jade. "For a long time I had no one else to go to anyway." She sipped her tea, looking away once again. "But, if this hadn't happened," she said slowly, almost inaudibly, "I think I would have left him soon."

Jade leaned forward, intrigued. Perhaps she did have someone else to run to. Was that what she was holding back from Jade? From Stevie? "Did you ever love him, Vanessa?"

Vanessa hesitated so long Jade thought she wasn't going to answer. When she looked at Jade, her eyes were moist and unmasked. "Of course not. Not after you . . ."

Jade smiled to herself and felt a small sense of vindication. But she didn't want to go there, didn't want to dredge up the ugly part of their past. It was so much water under the bridge, it was enough to drown an army. It wasn't worth Jade's effort to explain how, to her at least, their old relationship was nothing compared with what Jade had now with Stevie.

"Surely there must have been someone in all those

years," Jade quietly suggested, "who captured your interest, who made you feel *something*."

Vanessa's eyes fixed on an invisible horizon, the cup cradled between both hands. Jade saw the tiny tremble in her fingers.

Yes, Jade thought, I've hit on something here. "C'mon, Vanessa, I know you. I know what you need, remember? And if you weren't getting it from James, you must have been getting it somewhere."

Vanessa's smile was one of irony, not joy. "Oh, I got plenty elsewhere. I've had my share of men and women, Jade."

"And?"

Vanessa set the cup down with an awkward clink. Her trembling hand rose to her face, brushed her forehead, rested uncertainly over her eyes. "Oh god, Jade." She hunched over in a sudden fit of sobs, tears streaming through her fingers and down her face.

Jade pushed her chair beside Vanessa's and clasped her arm around her. "It's okay, Vanessa, whatever it is."

Vanessa sobbed and shook like a wounded animal. She muttered, her words tumbling into one another as though they couldn't get out fast enough. "I love her so much, Jade. All I want is to be with her and I can't. We can't. We'll never . . . oh god." She choked on more tears, her voice cracking. "It's so damned hopeless."

Jade hugged Vanessa closer, smoothed her hair. "Maybe it's not so hopeless," she whispered. "Tell me about her."

CHAPTER FIVE

Jade knew something was wrong the instant she entered the dark house. Tonka's greeting was exuberant and almost desperate, as though she'd been ignored for hours. She led Jade, as though tattling on a sibling, to a sleeping Stevie, curled up crookedly in a leather wing chair. Jade frowned at the empty whiskey bottle on the floor, then at the crumpled, snoring heap in front of her.

Stevie didn't drink hard liquor much any more unless she'd had a very bad day. Jade felt a surge of concern and a healthy dose of guilt for having been away.

Jade tenderly brushed the hair from Stevie's forehead and kissed her. "Honey, wake up. I'm home now. Stevie, c'mon, honey, let's go up to bed."

Stevie stirred in a fight against consciousness, then finally her eyes fluttered open. There was an instant of hesitation, of focusing. Then Stevie leapt up like a cobra unfurling, rattling a fistful of papers at Jade, her face in shadows.

There was no mistaking the anger constricting Stevie's voice. "You lied to me, Jade," she hissed. "You've been lying to me all along!"

Jade felt stunned, reached to turn on a lamp, then wished she hadn't when she saw the ugly rage contorting Stevie's face.

"I don't know what you're talking about, Stevie," she answered calmly. "Why don't you tell me."

The papers were thrust at her again and Jade took them, scanned them quickly. *Shit*. She hadn't realized she still had these stupid letters; she should have destroyed them a long time ago.

"Stevie," she soothed. "There's nothing —"

"You're still in love with her!" Stevie shot back, brimming with bitterness and blame, her voice low, uncompromising. "I bet you've been fucking her too. Is that how you've been comforting her?"

Jade slapped Stevie hard across the face, the sting on her hand surprising her, shocking Jade into a reality she would give anything to reverse.

They both stood frozen, slowly absorbing the violence of their confrontation. Neither had ever hit the other before. Jade's hand flew to her face, her eyes widening with each silent, painful second of realization.

"Oh god, Stevie," she gasped. "I never meant —"

Stevie turned and sprinted up the stairs. A slamming door reverberated through the house. Jade sat down where Stevie had been asleep just moments ago, resting her tear-stained face in her hands, not quite believing what she had just done. She cried from the fear and worry they might not be able to recover from this.

Stevie had dashed out of the house at dawn to avoid Jade. They'd slept in separate rooms — another first — and now Stevie had left, taking an overnight bag with her. She had no intention of going back to the house tonight, not until Jade got herself together and figured out what — who — the hell she wanted.

Stevie was well into her third cup of coffee by the time Jovanowski entered the third-floor squad room.

"You look like hell, Houston. What'd you do, sleep out in the doghouse last night?"

Stevie gave her partner an I'm-not-in-the-mood glare and handed him a piece of paper with a dozen names, addresses, and phone numbers all neatly typed out.

"What's this?"

"The names of all the people who work at Hedley's investment firm. I was over there early this morning. Scooped the human resources person when she got out of her car."

Jovanowski smiled in wonderment. "How'd you get her to give you all this without a warrant?"

Stevie forced a smile to mask the absolute torture she felt inside over Jade. "She was cute and I brought her the best damned cup of coffee you can find in this city."

Jovanowski frowned and shook his head. "I gotta learn some of that Houston charm, I guess."

"Still not back with Jocelyn?"

Jovanowski grunted absently as he read the list. "I can start with this guy at the top, this Lemming. He's the firm's accountant, huh?"

Stevie put her feet up on her desk and leaned back in her chair. "I already have an appointment to talk to him in" — she glanced at her watch — "twenty minutes."

"Jesus, Stevie, it's only nine in the friggin' morning. What are you, Wonder Woman?"

Stevie smiled at the compliment. She relished the respect of an old veteran and a good cop like Jovanowski, no matter how disguised it was. Gradually, he'd been handing over the reins to her more and more in their work together. He was getting closer to retirement, and it was becoming more obvious to Stevie that Jovanowski, in his unassuming, gruff way, was grooming her to take a more prominent role in the homicide department.

"Sorry, but I like to think of myself more as the Bionic Woman. Somehow I don't think I'd suit that tight, skimpy outfit Wonder Woman wears."

Jovanowski was studying the list again. "I'll go over there and start at the bottom of this thing. How's that?"

"Good." Stevie pulled a copy of the *Financial Post* from her drawer. "I've been reading up on Hedley Investors. 'Course, it's almost put me to sleep reading all this business crap. It —" Stevie glanced up at Jovanowski, who looked positively depressed all of the sudden. "What?"

Jovanowski shrugged her question away. "Nothin'. Go on."

"The company looks healthy on paper. It went public a year ago — probably so Hedley could get some more cash. And the share prices on the TSE have been holding steady. But," Stevie emphasized by stabbing her pen in the air, "there were rumors in the local business community that Hedley's expensive lifestyle had outgrown his means. He was covering it, but who knows how long he could have kept getting away with it."

"How'd you get all this out of the newspaper?"

Stevie stood up, tossed the newspaper in her briefcase. "My neighbor Rick is a reporter at the *Post*. He doesn't know any more specifics about Hedley or the company, but it's enough to give me some leverage with this Roger Lemming weasel."

"How do you figure he's a weasel?"

Stevie laughed. "Aren't all accountants?"

Stevie was expecting a short, thin, bespectacled, geeky middle-aged man when she knocked on Roger Lemming's office door. What awaited her was quite unexpected.

Roger Lemming was tall and muscled, and his long blond hair was tied back in a ponytail. His tanned face sported a mustache and goatee. He greeted Stevie warmly enough — his smile was wide and well practiced, and his handshake was firm but warm. He was younger than she expected too — late thirties, she guessed.

Stevie tried to wipe the surprise from her face with a well-timed cough.

"Yeah, I know, you probably expected me to look different." Lemming laughed as he sat down in his chair, draping his leg over the arm. Stevie sensed a man with an instinct to flirt with women. "Most people think accountants are all dweebs."

Stevie smiled. "You got me there. Pretty casual place here, is it?" Lemming's tight designer jeans, leather ankle boots and cotton collarless shirt hadn't gone unnoticed.

"Casual is our middle name here. James Hedley liked us all to feel like we were one big, happy family." He grinned, a glimmer of mischief in his sky blue eyes.

"And were you?" Stevie asked.

Lemming folded smooth, manicured hands on the desktop. "Sure. Mostly everyone here likes a good party, and Jimmy sure knew how to throw one."

Stevie opened her notebook, pen poised. "Were you at his house last Friday night? The night he died?"

"Yeah, I was at the party. I didn't get there till late, probably close to midnight."

"Were a lot of people there?"

Lemming settled back in his chair, glancing periodically at the ceiling as he recalled the night. "About three dozen people, I guess. Lots of music, lots of booze, you know . . . Everybody was having a good time."

Stevie looked up from her notebook. "Drugs?"

Lemming stared back, crossed his arms over his sculpted chest, and hesitated as though weighing what he would say next. It didn't take him long. "Look, Detective Houston —"

"Stevie," she interrupted, wanting to cultivate this witness on a more personal level.

"All right, Stevie," he smiled. "Cool name. Anyway, I know you're going to go back to your office and check up on me." Lemming winked. "If you haven't already." He reached for a small mahogany humidor on his desk and lifted the lid. "Would you like a cigar with me, Stevie?"

Stevie couldn't contain a smile. A man after her own heart. "Sure."

He made his selections, clipped the ends off both, and handed one to Stevie. "A Macanudo Petite Corona," he said proudly and held a Blazer lighter up to first hers, than his own.

"Excellent choice," Stevie remarked, knowing the little Jamaican gems were both pricey and delicious. She didn't make a practice of buying such expensive cigars herself, so this was a real treat.

"As I was about to say," he resumed after an appreciative puff, "it won't be any secret to you that I have a conviction from two years ago of cocaine possession."

Stevie admired his candor — finally, a witness in this case who wasn't trying to hide something. She hadn't yet done a records check on Roger Lemming, but he had been right in guessing that she would. "I see," Stevie answered objectively. "Your conviction isn't a problem for you?"

Lemming smiled between puffs. "I like to have a good time once in a while, that's all. I don't sell it and I don't do the stuff every day, so what the hell."

"Look, Roger, if you expect me to admonish you

for it, I'm afraid you'll be disappointed. Personally, I don't give a shit what you or anyone else does on their own time, as long as it's not hurting anyone."

Lemming shook his head, a grin splashed across his square-jawed good looks. "I never thought I'd hear *that* from a cop."

"You probably don't know many cops," Stevie replied. If he did, he'd know that most cops weren't law enforcement fanatics. They were everyday people with all the faults and habits of everyone else. "The party." Stevie took a luxurious puff on her cigar. "Did you know everyone there?"

"Most, but there were a handful I didn't know. Not unusual with Hedley, though."

"How's that?"

Lemming shrugged nonchalantly. "He always had a few hookers at these things, sometimes a drug dealer or two, people like that."

Stevie scribbled in her notebook without looking up. "Did Hedley do many drugs?"

"He snorted coke once in awhile, smoked dope. That's about it."

"Heroin?"

"Never."

Stevie looked up, her pen frozen mid-stroke. "Did he ever inject coke?"

Lemming adamantly shook his head, his lips pursed.

"How can you be so sure?"

Lemming set his cigar in a silver-plated ashtray, his hands moving in staccato expression. "He hated needles. He had a real needle phobia. Whenever he had to get a blood test or an allergy shot or something, somebody from the office would have to drive him in case he passed out. And he always said he never had any use for heroin. He considered it a hard drug, and he didn't want anything to do with hard drugs."

Stevie considered Lemming's words. She was pleased for the added confirmation that James Hedley could not have injected the fatal drugs into his body. "Did anyone at the party behave suspiciously?"

Lemming thought for a moment, then shook his head. "Nothing that struck me. Everyone was just doing their own thing, you know: drinking, a few drugs, making out."

Stevie sighed to herself. Definitely not her type of party. "Was there anyone there who would want to do James Hedley any harm?"

Lemming's smile was meant to be condescending, to point out Stevie's naiveté. "Look, I'm not going to paint you some rosy, phony picture of Hedley. The guy was selfish, a boor really, and he'd use people if there was something he wanted from you. But he had balls. You always knew where you stood with him, and if he liked you, he'd stick by you." Lemming winked. "And he could throw a helluva party."

Stevie frowned. Roger Lemming, it seemed, had a nose for a good party. Probably not much else in life mattered to him. "You didn't answer my question, Roger. Did he have enemies?"

"Of course," Lemming answered incredulously. "He couldn't have built a successful company like this without running over a few people. Let's face it, the guy pissed people off."

"Enough for someone to kill him?"

Lemming picked up his cigar again and studied it as though it were some piece of fine art. "I guess that's for you to find out, eh, Detective?" He looked at her, then softened his expression, either out of remorse for his comment or because he really did want to help; Stevie couldn't be sure. "Guys like James Hedley are a dime a dozen. There're all kinds of pricks out there like him, but I don't think he was worse than any of the rest of them."

Stevie nodded slowly. James Hedley had obviously pissed off someone enough to retaliate by killing him. "Do you have any thoughts whatsoever on who the killer might be or why?"

Lemming thought for a moment, then leaned over the desk as though he were about to tell her a secret. "Look, James Hedley had a weakness for coke and chicks. I mean, the guy died of an overdose, right? He probably went up to his room with some broad to have a good time and things got out of hand. Maybe she overdosed him by accident and was too scared to stick around."

Stevie hadn't yet told him that it was a combination of injected coke and heroin — enough, if toxicology tests confirmed what Jade thought — to kill a horse. Far too extravagant for just having a good time. She decided to change the subject. "What kind of financial health is this company in?"

Lemming shrugged noncommitally, sucked on his cigar. "It's doing fine."

"That's not what I heard," Stevie suggested coyly. "I understand James Hedley was in trouble financially."

Lemming coughed, looking uncomfortable, then smiled reluctantly. "Are you just fishing or do you know something, Stevie?"

Stevie held her ground and ignored the question.

"Hedley had an expensive lifestyle. Cars, vacations, a nice house, an expensive wife, parties. I'm guessing he had girlfriends. He'd have to be a financial genius for this company to be pulling in that much money, and frankly I just don't see it."

"How do you figure that?" Lemming asked coolly.

"Share prices are steady, but at nine-fifty a share, that's hardly the big leagues." Stevie leveled a merciless glare at Roger Lemming. Time to play hardball. "Are you going to tell me where he was getting his money? Or do I have to get a forensic accountant in here to rip through all your books?"

Stevie settled back in her chair, puffed her cigar, and let her threat hover over the suddenly squirming accountant. "Of course, if the word got out to shareholders that we were ripping this place apart, that wouldn't do much for the share price, would it?"

Lemming stared back, his cigar back in the ashtray, his hands clasped tightly on the desktop.

"I assume you have shares yourself in this company, no?" Stevie continued.

Lemming nodded almost imperceptibly.

"Then I'm sure you don't want to see the prices tumble."

Lemming drew a deep breath. "Boy, you sure know how to grab a guy by the balls. I almost admire that. You ever think of going into the business world?"

Stevie shook her head. Her father was a corporate lawyer in Calgary, Alberta. Her older brother and sister had followed in his footsteps while Stevie, the black sheep, was the only cop in the family.

Lemming relaxed back in his chair again, glanced out the window of his sixth floor downtown office, then swung his gaze back to Stevie. He was clear eyed and firm, but his face was suddenly ashen. "You're right. Hedley couldn't keep up with his lifestyle the last couple of years. We juggled budgets, temporarily 'borrowed' money from our clients's accounts against their interest, trying to eke out a few bucks. I stayed awake plenty of nights trying to figure out legal ways to get him more money." He shook his head resignedly. "If he hadn't been so money hungry, this place could have been really hopping. I did what I could, but he was never happy with it."

Stevie stroked her chin contemplatively. "But he didn't cut back on his lifestyle, did he?"

Lemming stood up, stretched, then sat on the corner of his desk in front of Stevie, his tight jeans hugging his body, his boyish, lopsided smile exposing gleaming white teeth. If Stevie didn't know better, he was working up to asking her out. "No ma'am, he liked to live the high life."

"So where was he getting his money?"

Lemming shrugged, all nonchalance. "I really didn't want to know, and he didn't tell me."

Stevie ripped a blank page from her notebook and handed it to Lemming. "Can you do me a favor and write down the names of the people you knew at the party?"

"Anything for you, Stevie," he grinned again, then began writing.

Stevie set her expired cigar in the ashtray. "Thanks again for the Macanudo."

"Any time. Maybe some time we can get together and trade sticks?" He leered at her. "I'll show you mine if you show me yours."

Stevie shook her head, smiling. "Roger, that's the worse pickup line I've ever heard. And the answer's no."

Lemming sighed, his eyes probing her body. "Too bad. I've always wanted to do a cop."

Stevie laughed, too amused to be irritated, and collected the piece of paper from Lemming. She stood up to go. "One more thing. What do think of Vanessa Hedley?"

Lemming slid off the desk and onto his feet. "Sexy broad, huh? Boy, she's hot."

She's hot all right, Stevie thought. *Burns every goddamned thing she touches.* "Do you know her well?"

Lemming shrugged. "Not really. I think she just basically did her own thing. Didn't much care for her husband's parties, I know that much."

Stevie held her business card out to him. "I'll be in touch again."

"Looking forward to it."

CHAPTER SIX

Stevie ravenously consumed her tuna melt and fries while, across from her, Ted Jovanowski devoured his steak and potatoes like a man rebounding from a coerced vegetarian diet. It had been a long day interviewing James Hedley's employees, and the late dinner was the first chance the two detectives had had to trade information.

They compared mental notes between welcome gulps of beer. All of the employees questioned agreed that James Hedley had been a pig. Promiscuous, chauvinistic, recreational drug user, alcoholic, wily, manipulative. But he was a hell of a businessman, they all said. He always found a way to come up with a buck. None knew of any enemies who would have reason to take him out, unless plain dislike or contempt were enough.

"Next we get to tackle that list of partygoers," Stevie groaned, already exhausted by the thought of the endless legwork still ahead.

"There is one more juicy tidbit I almost forgot to tell you," Jovanowski mumbled through a mouth full of chocolate cake. He put his hand up like a stop sign. "I know, I know, Jade would kill me if she saw me eating this stuff. She'd be telling me I was on my way to another heart attack."

Stevie mentally winced at Jade's name. She had done her best all day to ignore the heart sickening developments of the night before. She'd ignored the three urgent phone messages from Jade that had been left on her desk. But now she felt the pain, sharp as a knife, ripping at the center of her gut. In her mind she replayed their fight, felt the sting all over again from Jade's slap.

"So?" Joavanowski demanded. "You want to hear it or what?"

Stevie shook herself from her thoughts. "Yeah, yeah, your juicy tidbit."

"Your accountant, Lemming. It looks like studman had a go with Vanessa Hedley a couple of years back."

Stevie felt her mouth slacken in surprise. "That little prick. Should have known his friendly cooperation was too good to be true. He told me he hardly knew Vanessa."

"According to Linda Estrella, Hedley's personal

secretary, Mr. Lemming knew Mrs. Hedley pretty damn good. In the biblical sense."

"Shit," Stevie muttered and sipped her beer. "I'm going to have to go see him again. I don't like that he's holding out on me."

"Think he's got something else to hide?"

Stevie shrugged. "I don't know what he's got up his sleeve. But we've got to nail down any possible stray motives out there, and a little love triangle is definitely not putting my mind at ease."

Each sipped their drinks in silent contemplation. Half a beer later, Jovanowski cleared his throat. He set his beer mug down with a thump.

"Stevie," he said slowly, almost reluctantly. "We need to talk about something."

Stevie looked up in alarm. Jovanowski wasn't much of a conversationalist.

"We gotta talk about me retiring soon. My doc says if I want to collect my pension, I better think about getting out in the next few months."

Stevie nodded slowly. Ted Jovanowski was almost fifty-eight years old now. Like all cops in the province, he would be mandatorily required to retire at the age of sixty. The fact that he would be going earlier wasn't a total surprise to Stevie, especially in light of his heart attack more than two years ago. But her having already sensed where he was going made it no easier.

He glumly studied his beer. "It's all I've known since I was twenty years old. No matter what else, I always had my job."

Stevie had gathered that his stubborn dedication to his job had cost him his marriage years ago, though

71

he'd never spoken of it. He had no children and not many friends. The prospect of him being all alone, with no hobbies and no friends, scared the hell out of Stevie.

"You'll be okay, Ted," Stevie reassured, her words ringing hollow to her own ears at least. She really had no idea whether or not Jovanowski would be okay. "Maybe you could go into private detective work, or be a crime consultant, or maybe even teach. And there's always traveling."

When Jovanowski looked up, there were tears in his eyes. "I'm losing it, Tex."

Stevie smiled at the old nickname he used for her. He began calling her Tex on their first case together two and a half years ago. She'd hated it at first.

"What are you talking about?"

He blinked his eyes. "I see it in you, when we work together on a case, I . . ."

"Ted, you're not making any sense."

"You've got it and I don't any more, Stevie. I feel like I'm holding you back."

Stevie reached across the table for his hand and clasped it. "Ted, that's nonsense," she replied forcefully. "You've taught me everything. You're still the best."

He shook his head. "No, kid, you've jumped way ahead of me. I'm gettin' out while I should. I figure this'll be my last big case."

Stevie released his hand to wipe the tears in her own eyes. They were both silent for a while, lost in their own thoughts and in their beer glasses.

Jovanowski spoke first. "The rumors are true around the office about getting rid of the two-man teams."

Stevie looked up, instantly intrigued. She'd heard that soon there would be teams of three homicide detectives investigating every case, with one of the three being the supervising detective.

"I'm recommending to the inspector that you be one of the leads. I think you're ready."

"Oh, Ted," Stevie began to protest. "No, I couldn't, not yet."

Jovanowski held up a hand. "You will, and you'll be great."

Stevie was lost for words, wishing she could rush home and talk to Jade about her fears, her excitement at the challenges ahead. But she couldn't. Not tonight. "You're really going to do this, aren't you?" Stevie said softly while Jovanowski simply nodded. "Does any of this have to do with the problems you and Jocelyn are having?" She figured while he was being so open, she might as well go for broke.

Jovanowski shrugged. "I just need time to deal with this by myself right now, and she's bugging me to move in together.

Stevie smiled. She liked Jocelyn and knew she and Jovanowski cared deeply for one another. "You should do it, Ted. I think it'd be great."

He shrugged again, sheepishly staring into the beer mug he gripped between both hands. "Yeah, she's pretty great. But I'm not ready yet. It's been a long time since I've lived with anybody."

Stevie nodded and felt her mind tunneling into her own problems with Jade. She felt nauseous. If Jade had re-ignited an affair with Vanessa, Stevie would not be able to forgive her. She could not allow Jade to hurt her like that.

"Are you going to tell me what's going on with you

and Jade? 'Cause I ain't gonna be the only one to sit here and spill my guts."

Stevie smiled, touched by this newfound intimacy. But she just couldn't tell Jovanowski about Vanessa Hedley being Jade's old girlfriend, and of her suspicions that they'd re-ignited their affair. She didn't want to be pulled off the case, and she didn't want Jade to get in trouble either. In spite of her hurt, Stevie still felt protective of her lover.

"It's no big deal," Stevie lied. "Just a little bump on the road to paradise." She dug around in her pocket for her car keys. "It's been a long day, Ted. I've got to get some sleep." She stood to go and didn't tell her partner she was off to search for a hotel for the night.

Stevie had arrived early at James Hedley's Bloor Street office, with Hedley's own office the first item on her agenda. She'd sent a uniformed cop around after the autopsy to seal Hedley's office. His staff had been complaining ever since that it was hindering the operation of the company. It was quiet this morning though. Everyone was at the funeral, Stevie guessed.

Stevie removed the sticky police tape sealing the door. Sitting in James Hedley's leather chair, she looked around the cluttered surroundings. It reminded her of her own jumbled life right now. There was still Jade to deal with, and the truth, however unpleasant it might be, of their future together. And the case itself was still in the infancy stage, with so much more work to be done. Jovanowski was starting to interview the partygoers, but it would take them at least a couple of days to get through everyone. Crime scene reports from the police lab would be ready any day and would require Stevie's scrutiny. Same with tox reports on Hedley from the Center of Forensic Sciences. Lemming had to be reinterviewed, as would just about every other witness they'd already talked to, just in case someone remembered something later on. And Vanessa would have to be investigated more thoroughly.

Stevie rubbed her eyes — she hadn't slept much at the hotel — took a sip of the coffee she'd brought with her, and contemplated where to begin.

She switched on Hedley's computer, opening all the files she could find. She was no computer goddess, and if he'd wanted to hide things within certain files, she'd probably never find them. Next she opened his email program and spent the next forty minutes studying his outgoing and ingoing personal mail. Nothing. Nada. A big fat zero.

Stevie then carefully went through the desk drawers and later the filing cabinets. There was nothing suspicious, no scrap of paper outlining some secret, dubious meeting, no threatening letters. Nothing.

Stevie glanced at her watch. She'd been searching the office for three hours and felt hunger pangs. There was only one thing left to search: the briefcase on the floor of the office closet.

Stevie snapped open the unlocked briefcase and was quickly disappointed. There were pamphlets about stocks, two quarterly reports from mutual fund companies, a book called *The Secret to Good Investing*. She emptied the contents and studied the briefcase itself, making sure she hadn't missed anything. She dug through the leather pockets, then turned the case upside down and shook it. She heard a muffled rattling, put her ear closer and shook it again. Same noise.

Stevie righted the briefcase and tapped the bottom with her pen. Sure enough, there was a hollow sound. A secret compartment. It took her a few minutes to find the latch, which was disguised as a staple remover. Stevie felt like a kid at Christmas and eagerly lifted the lid of the compartment. Inside was a brown envelope.

Carefully, she opened the envelope with her pen knife and gently let the contents — five eight-by-ten photos — fall over her lap. Stevie smiled and shook her head. *Good ol' Vanessa, caught in the act.* The photos all depicted Vanessa and an unidentified, younger woman engaged in various forms of embrace and undress in the back seat of a car. The photos obviously had been taken with a long lens.

Vanessa was one busy woman, Stevie thought amusedly. An affair with Roger Lemming and now proof of an affair with a woman, of which James Hedley was obviously well aware. Stevie removed a plastic evidence bag from her own briefcase, stuck the photos in the bag, and labeled it. The curious part was, what was James Hedley doing with the photos? Was he being blackmailed? Or was he blackmailing the unidentified woman or perhaps her husband?

There was a knock on the closed door.

"Come in," Stevie called out, clicking her briefcase shut.

Roger Lemming stood in the doorway, dressed in a black suit, white shirt, and dark red tie. Clean shaven and neat, there was still something subtly unkempt about him, as if he hadn't slept much. "I heard you were here."

Stevie nodded. "How did the funeral go?"

Lemming shrugged. "Fine. Not many people there. Guess most of his party friends have forgotten him already."

"I need to talk to you," Stevie said, leveling an unequivocal glare at him. This time, there would be no friendly banter.

"Sure," Lemming shrugged again. "Why don't you come to my office."

Stevie followed him and took the same seat she'd sat in just yesterday. She watched him shed his jacket and rip off his tie. He seemed much more sullen than he'd been yesterday.

"So what do you want to talk to me about?"

"I want to talk about why you lied to me yesterday."

Lemming sat down in his chair and closed his bloodshot eyes briefly. When he looked at Stevie again there was resignation in his face. Perhaps, Stevie decided, Roger Lemming was beginning to unravel.

"I need a drink. Want one?"

Stevie declined with a shake of her head as Lemming reached behind him to open a small wood cabinet. He pulled out a glass and a bottle of seven-year-old Cuban rum. He filled the glass, returned the bottle, and took a leisurely sip.

He certainly liked the finer things, Stevie thought. Expensive cigars, expensive rum. She'd also noticed a pricey bottle of Rémy Martin cognac in the opened cabinet.

Stevie broke his introspection. "I understand you knew Vanessa Hedley better than you led me to believe."

He stared at her, hints of a smile tugging at his narrow mouth. "I knew her awhile ago, a couple of years ago."

"Did you have an affair with her?"

Lemming nodded after a few seconds, tried to look casual with a shrug. "Yeah, I slept with her a few times. What can I say, she's a beautiful woman, a very sexual woman. And great in bed."

Stevie grimaced, unable to keep the pictures from forming in her head of Vanessa and Jade making love. It sickened her, and she felt the anger rising in her. She wished now she could have taken that drink.

"Hedley didn't mind that you were screwing his wife?"

Lemming laughed. "Hell no, he got off on it." He leaned forward and winked at Stevie. "I hear she's even done it with women."

Stevie ignored his last comment. "Why didn't you tell me before about this affair?"

Lemming's voice dropped to a near whisper. "Look, I read in the paper that Vanessa's a suspect. I just didn't want to make things worse for her. I mean, it's private stuff. And Vanessa and I, well, it was a long time ago, and it was cool with all of us."

Stevie reached into her briefcase and retrieved the evidence bag containing the photos of Vanessa making love to a young, dark-haired woman. She splayed the photos across his desk.

"Did he get off on this, too?"

Lemming looked at the pictures, looked up at Stevie, swallowed hard. His face had suddenly paled like a blank piece of paper. "Where did you get these?"

"I'm not at liberty to say. It's evidence now. Do you know who she is?" Stevie pointed to the anonymous woman in the photo.

Lemming inhaled deeply in an effort to compose himself. "Sorry, I don't know anything about this or who this is."

Stevie stood up and gathered the photos together. She knew Roger Lemming was lying to her.

"If you do suddenly remember something about these pictures, I can help you."

He looked puzzled. "What do you mean?"

Stevie snapped her briefcase shut. "If these photos are tied to the killer somehow, you could be in danger if you know anything about them."

Lemming babbled nervously. "Look, I, I'd help if I could. I just, I don't know anything more."

Stevie winked knowingly at him, as if his secret was out, and left him looking like a frightened little boy.

CHAPTER SEVEN

It was dark as Stevie drove the few blocks from police headquarters on College Street to the four-story, Victorian-style duplex she shared with Jade on Sackville Street in Toronto's Cabbagetown. It was an old, once-moneyed neighborhood that was now considered tony in an endearing, earthy sort of way. It was a yuppie haven with a large population of gays and lesbians.

It felt good to wend her way home. It'd been forty-eight hours since her blowout with Jade — enough time, she hoped, for them to talk reasonably about what had happened; to sort things out.

As Stevie parked her convertible Mustang and pulled up on the hand brake, she felt a twinge of panic in her gut that was quickly threatening to become all-consuming. What if Jade didn't want her anymore? What if she wanted Vanessa instead? Stevie was afraid of what awaited, yet she knew she couldn't hide forever.

How is it, she wondered as she trudged heavily up the interlocking brick walkway, that she could stare down the wrong end of a gun and feel less fearful than she did now.

The door was unlocked — a good sign. Tonka charged up to her, and Stevie knelt to let the wiggling retriever lick her face.

Jade stood in the hallway and watched as Stevie stalled and avoided eye contact for as long as she could. Finally, she stood and shrugged out of her nylon jacket. "Hi."

Jade rushed to Stevie, almost knocking her backward as she collapsed into her, wrapping her arms around her.

"Oh, Stevie," Jade sobbed. "I'm so sorry. I missed you so much. Please don't ever leave like that again."

Stevie held her lover tightly and felt tears of her own slither down her face. "I'm sorry too, baby."

They stood clutching each other for a while, until Jade began frantically kissing Stevie, crushing Stevie's mouth with her own, her hands roughly pawing at the buttons of Stevie's shirt.

"Whoa, wait a minute, honey," Stevie pleaded, gently taking Jade's hands and kissing them tenderly.

"I just want you so much," Jade cried.

"And I want to make love to you too, but we need to talk first."

Jade reluctantly agreed and held hands with Stevie as they walked to the living room, where a fire was roaring in the fireplace and candlelight from just about every surface danced off the high ceiling.

"Did you know I was coming?" Stevie smiled for the first time in days.

Jade beamed in return. "I'd hoped."

They sat close on the love seat, Jade's shiny black hair, olive skin, sculpted cheekbones, and green eyes illuminated by the firelight. Jade had never looked more beautiful, Stevie breathed. She simply sparkled; Stevie's very own Indian goddess, there beside her again. Stevie felt enormous relief.

Tempted as she was to tear Jade's clothes off and leave the talking for later, Stevie took a deep breath, determined to have their talk first. Damn, it was hard, with that soft skin next to her own and the sexual tension between them pulsating like a beacon.

"Honey," Stevie whispered. "I need to know what's been going on with you and Vanessa."

"Oh, Stevie, there's been *nothing* going on."

"But, all the time you've been spending with her, and then when I found those letters . . ." Stevie couldn't finish, the memory still too bitter.

Jade traced an abstract design on Stevie's palm. Her touch was soft, electrifying. "Honey, I know. You had every right to feel the way you did after you read those stupid things. I didn't even know I still had them."

Stevie swallowed and felt tears near the surface.

But she had to know. Her voice cracked. "Are you sleeping with her?"

A tear spilled down Jade's cheek. She pulled Stevie into her. "Oh god, Stevie."

Jade was crying again, and for an instant, Stevie feared the worst.

"No, I'm not sleeping with Vanessa. I've never been unfaithful to you."

Stevie wanted so badly to believe Jade, wanted it with every fiber of her body. She'd never loved or needed anyone this much before, and the thought of losing Jade was the most frightening thing she'd ever encountered. Even more frightening than the drowning death of her twin sister almost three decades ago.

She took mental stock of their marriage, the good times they'd had. Like the thrill of decorating the house for their first Christmas together and how they'd made love under the tree. The long evening walks with Tonka, the two of them holding hands; the leisurely Sunday mornings over coffee and the *Toronto Star*. And last winter's romantic trip to the Caribbean. Stevie wanted nothing more than a hell of a lot more good memories ahead.

Jade spoke through her tears again. "I love you, Stevie, with all my heart. I would never do anything to hurt you. The only thing Vanessa and I have done is talk."

Stevie held Jade tightly and felt all the tension and fear that had collected in her body for days evaporate into the softness of this gorgeous woman in her arms. She felt foolish now for doubting Jade's love for her.

"I'm sorry for being suspicious, Jade. I just love

you to death." Stevie choked out the words, her chest tighter than a mile-high kite. "I don't know what I'd do without you."

"Well, that's one thing you won't have to find out." Jade found Stevie's lips and kissed her for all she was worth. This time Stevie didn't try to stop Jade's frenetic hands and mouth as she tried to consume Stevie and meld their bodies together.

"I love you," Jade murmured before her tongue darted into Stevie's parted mouth, her lips and hands voracious in their mission. She tore at Stevie's shirt, popping the buttons, as she straddled her lap. Her hands roughly jerked Stevie's breasts free and she cupped them, her thumbs massaging Stevie's nipples to life.

Stevie pulled away from Jade's mouth and grinned up at her. "I like you when you're wild." Jade was half Indian, half French, and Stevie loved the hot-blooded combination. "I could get used to this."

Jade ended the conversation with another lip lock. Her hands slid down to her satin pajama bottoms, and she pulled the silky material down her muscular, compact thighs. She was naked underneath, and in response, Stevie felt that oh-so-familiar ache between her legs. Her hands cupped Jade's firm, round ass, and she pulled her up into her chest, their mouths parting. Stevie inhaled deeply as Jade's soft mound pressed into her breasts. Stevie clutched Jade to her chest, felt her nipples harden at the gyrating, wet nakedness slathering her skin.

Jade began to slither farther up, Stevie squeezing

her eyes shut, afraid she might come right then and there. God, she had missed Jade.

Stevie reached for her own crotch, still imprisoned in denim, and was determined to relieve the throbbing tension there. But Jade would have none of it. She grabbed Stevie's hands and planted them on her naked hips as she knelt against her, slowly riding farther up until her plush wetness pushed against Stevie's mouth.

Oh yes! Stevie thought as her mouth impulsively began to explore the soft, swollen, cherry red folds of flesh. Tenderly, Stevie's lips kissed and caressed the gift she'd been given. She delighted in Jade's soft moaning and pulled her tight to her mouth. They pressed against each other, Stevie's mouth taking in all of Jade, sucking, swallowing Jade's juices. They were going at it full throttle, the same way they had fought two nights ago.

"Oh, Stevie," Jade groaned in ragged breaths. She whispered fiercely, "I'm going to come."

"Not yet," Stevie commanded and jammed her tongue deep into Jade, tightly gripping Jade's hips, the stronger Stevie clasping her so that she could not go anywhere until Stevie was good and ready to let her. Jade threw her head back, her long, smooth neck exposed, satin outlined breasts circling above Stevie, hardened nipples poking through. Stevie ground Jade into her greedy mouth as her tongue thrust quick and hard, driving into Jade over and over again. Jade groaned loudly, her breaths short and quick, her chest heaving.

Oh yes, honey, Stevie thought. *Come to me. Give me all you've got.*

Stevie slid her right hand along Jade's bottom, withdrew her tongue and thrust two fingers into the warm passage that opened like a wide, warm river to welcome her. Jade moaned, deeper from her chest this time, and Stevie slipped a third finger in, pushing and pulling, gliding easily, filling Jade. Her tongue closed over Jade's clitoris, stiff and prominent in its quest for attention.

"Oh god!" Jade yelled out as her grinding hips strained, then stopped for a moment, as though she were on a precipice. She shuddered, then collapsed onto Stevie.

Softly, Jade began to cry as Stevie gently withdrew her fingers and lowered her onto her lap, where she could kiss away the wet tears.

Stevie hugged her lover, kissed her ear, her wet cheek. "It's okay, honey. I'm not going to let you go."

Jade smiled into Stevie's shoulder. "You were great, my love."

Stevie rocked Jade gently, as though she were a small child. "Everything's okay now, honey," she whispered. "We'll never fight like that again . . ." She looked at Jade, a gleam of mischief ascending in her eyes like a meteor. "Not unless we can make up like that again."

Jade laughed. "Let's not wait for a fight next time."

"Deal," Stevie laughed. "Now let's seal it with a kiss."

Jade was happy to comply, and they kissed long and passionately. Moments later, Jade's kisses began to trail down Stevie's neck, down to her strong shoulders and chest, Jade moving the cloth of her shirt aside to make way for her lips.

Stevie spontaneously arched her back as Jade's mouth found her left nipple, her hand closing in on and stroking Stevie's other nipple. Jade sucked gently and alternated between breasts until Stevie squirmed beneath her.

"You want more?" Jade teased, her eyebrows dancing suggestively.

Stevie was breathing hard, sweat beading on her forehead. She could only nod, her hand trailing down to her zipper, only to have Jade pull her hand away.

"That's my job," Jade answered. She tugged on Stevie's zipper, slid her hand inside Stevie's cotton boxers, her fingers becoming entangled in the web of soft hair.

"Oh, honey," Stevie breathed.

Jade pulled her hand out, much to Stevie's momentary consternation. Stevie felt she would burst at any second, and she reached for Jade's wandering hand again, aching for it to work its magic on her.

Jade took Stevie's hand and pulled her to the floor in front of the fireplace, Stevie complying like an obedient puppy. She knew Jade had her right now, had her eating from her very palm. She would do anything for Jade right now, say anything, give herself up to anything Jade wanted to do to her.

She lay on her back as Jade removed her jeans, then her boxers. Her tattered, sweat-soaked shirt was pulled aside, and Jade took a nipple in her mouth again, tugging gently. Stevie's body was rigid with pent-up want. She was so ripe, she felt she would explode like a volcano, her hot lava juices building and threatening to erupt.

"God, Jade," Stevie groaned impatiently. "Just fuck me, baby."

Jade responded with soft hands that found Stevie's desire, fingers plunging into her, taking and giving all at once. Stevie felt Jade's other hand close over the folds of her pounding flesh. Jade's hand pressed in hard circles as her fingers danced inside Stevie, pushing her to the edge and, finally, letting her fall gently over.

They lay in each other's arms, watching the flames lick the logs of wood. They basked in their love for each other, warmed by the moment, by the infinity of their love.

Jade stroked Stevie's face. "Honey, there's something I meant to tell you. Actually, I meant to tell you two nights ago when I came home, but then we had that terrible fight. And then I tried to call you at work all day yesterday to tell you."

Stevie propped herself up on her elbow, her forehead wrinkling with sudden worry. "Tell me what?"

"About who Vanessa's been seeing. She has a girl-friend."

Stevie exhaled deeply. The girl in the pictures. It had to be. "Who?"

"A young woman. Her name's Cheryl Myatt. They've been seeing each other for a few months, and it's pretty serious." Jade's voice grew more animated. "You see, it's why I've been spending so much time with Vanessa. I knew there was something she was hiding."

Stevie shook her head in wonder at Jade. "Jesus,

do I feel like a fool thinking you were trying to get back with Vanessa."

With her finger, Jade traced the outline of Stevie's lips. "Honey, getting back with Vanessa is the *last* thing I would ever want to do."

Grabbing Jade's finger, Stevie kissed it, then softly said: "But you loved each other at one time."

Jade stared at the fire and shook her head, a trace of sadness in her voice. "No, it wasn't love. We were in our early twenties. It was med school. We were far from home, exploring our sexuality, our independence. I really thought at the time it was some kind of love, but I know now it wasn't."

Stevie kissed Jade's finger again. "I'm sorry she hurt you."

Jade looked at Stevie, her eyes sparkling, her face still rosy from sex. "I won't pretend that I ever forgot her. But I've been over her for a long time."

"Is she the reason you married a man soon after that?" Stevie asked pensively.

Jade shrugged. "I don't know, maybe. It's more complicated than that, I guess." Jade leaned over and kissed the seriousness from Stevie's face. "All I care about now is you, us."

Stevie returned the kiss. "You're amazing."

"I know. So don't you want to hear more about this elusive girlfriend?"

Stevie smiled and caressed Jade's cheek. "I'm all ears, my love."

"They were spending the night together at a hotel when the murder happened."

"Shit. Why didn't Vanessa just tell us that?"

"She won't admit to it, not to you guys, anyway.

She's trying to protect Cheryl. She doesn't want her to have to testify in court about their relationship."

"You mean Vanessa would sooner go to prison for murder than have this relationship become public?" Stevie asked incredulously.

Jade shook her head. "Well, I don't know if she would carry it that far, but for now at least, she's going to protect Cheryl."

"Why? Protect her from what?"

Jade also propped herself up on her elbow, a mirror image of Stevie. "Doesn't the name Myatt mean anything to you?"

Stevie quirked her head, thought for a minute. "It does sound familiar. I've read it in the papers or something."

Jade nodded. "Jack Myatt's her dad. He's a local member of parliament for the Reform party. In fact, most of the political experts are predicting he'll be the next leader of the party once the next federal election is called. He'll be gunning for prime minister."

"Great," Stevie said, not happy. "So her dad's as far right on the political spectrum as you can get. Probably homophobic as hell. I can see he wouldn't be too happy about this whole thing getting into the press, especially if he's trying to make a national name for himself."

"Vanessa said Cheryl's having a fit over the whole thing. She's totally paranoid it'll ruin her family. You see, her brother Andy's a cookie-cutter image of their dad and wants to follow in his footsteps. The whole family's involved in politics. They'd never forgive her."

Stevie sat up.

"What are you doing?" Jade demanded.

"I'm going to go phone Ted about this."

Jade pulled Stevie back to the floor again. "Oh no you're not. It can wait til morning."

Stevie laughed and ran her hand along Jade's hip and across her smooth thigh. "You have plans to keep me busy tonight or something?"

Jade grinned. "You might say that. Come here."

CHAPTER EIGHT

Briefcase in hand, Stevie took the elevator to the second floor of the downtown building, to where the lobby's directory had indicated John Andrew Myatt's constituency office was located.

She stepped off the elevator and followed the signs down the plushly carpeted hallway until she came to the final sign and a set of large oak double doors left open for walk-in guests.

Stevie hadn't made an appointment, but she had called anonymously and was told Cheryl Myatt worked at the Toronto office as a special assistant to her father.

Just inside the office suite was a middle-aged woman at a desk completely made of glass. She looked up at Stevie, her hair, her face, tight like a mask. Her cat's eye glasses looked decades old. She tried to smile, as though as an afterthought, but the attempt made her face look like it might crack.

"Can I help you, miss?" Even her mannerisms were starched.

Stevie cleared her throat, buttoning her suit jacket to hide the pistol within. She would save her identity and the purpose of her visit for Cheryl. "I would like to see Cheryl Myatt, please. It's rather important."

Plucked eyebrows inched up. "May I ask who's here to see her and what it might be concerning?"

Stevie bit back a sarcastic retort. "I'm afraid it's personal. But as I said, it's rather urgent."

The woman hesitated in a mental game of cat and mouse that lasted mere seconds before she gave up and marched down the hallway behind her. Stevie noticed a door to her right, a gold-plated sign announcing it was the office of John Andrew Myatt, Member of Parliament. The door was closed and it was quiet, probably empty. As an MP, he would spend at least half of his time in the nation's capital, maybe more, Stevie knew. From down the hall Stevie could see that there were more offices.

Mrs. Bitch returned, a tall young woman behind her. The younger woman stepped in front and quickly extended a hand. It was her: the woman in the explicit photos with Vanessa Hedley. Stevie felt a pang of exhilaration. The case was starting to progress, the pieces at least forming a faint outline now, like a hazy shoreline along the water's horizon. Stevie and Jovanowski were no longer bobbing hopelessly.

"I'm Cheryl Myatt, can I help you?"

Stevie smiled back and shook the slender hand. She could understand why Vanessa would be attracted to the long-legged beauty before her. Her doelike eyes were a rich, dark brown, her short brown hair thick and very wavy, her smile warm, relaxed. Stevie had to hand it to Vanessa; she sure knew how to pick gorgeous women.

"I would like to speak privately to you, Ms. Myatt."

An audible sigh of exasperation escaped from the nameless receptionist, but Cheryl Myatt showed no irritation at Stevie's cryptic presence. She quirked her head in acquiescence, smiled again, and led Stevie down the hallway to her office.

They passed a door that was part open, a name-plate on it indicating the office belonged to Andrew Zachary Myatt. The ambitious brother, Stevie gathered. There were muffled sounds from within. He was there. Stevie began to doubt her decision to come here, thinking it might have been better to take Cheryl to a coffee shop — anywhere but here — for privacy. But they were suddenly in her office, and Cheryl Myatt smiled at Stevie again, totally oblivious to the fact that her whole world was about to change.

"Please, have a seat, Ms . . ."

Stevie sat down on the cushy, flower-patterned love seat in the corner of the large office. Orange light glowed from the gas fireplace adjacent to the love seat, the setting more like a living room than an office. Stevie set her briefcase beside her. "Thank you. I'm Stephanie Houston. Everyone calls me Stevie."

The faintest look of puzzlement crept into the soft, fine features of Cheryl's face. It wasn't in her to be rude, to demand what this stranger in her office wanted. Well-bred, Stevie mused. Cheryl pointed to a cabinet in the corner where a freshly brewed pot of coffee stood, the enticing aroma filling the room.

"Coffee?" she asked pleasantly.

Stevie nodded. "That would be wonderful. Just black, please."

She watched Cheryl retrieve two mugs from the cabinet and pour the brew into them. She moved like a thoroughbred, Stevie thought. All grace, subtle confidence, sexy without even trying to be. Her clothes — black pin-striped skirt and matching jacket, pale pink silk blouse — accentuated her perfect lines, exposed just enough of the trim but well-toned legs without being tasteless. She was young — twenty-six as of two months ago, Stevie had found out from running her name through the Ministry of Transportation's vehicle licensing system.

Stevie accepted the steaming mug. "Thank you."

Cheryl Myatt, crossing her long legs, sat in a matching wing chair opposite Stevie. Her forehead told Stevie she was perplexed, even a little nervous, as though she were beginning to clue in to the serious subject matter hanging over them. "What is it that I can do for you, Stevie?"

Stevie set her cup on the coffee table in front of her. She spoke quietly. "Actually, Ms. Myatt, I —"

"Please, call me Cheryl." She laughed nervously.

Stevie nodded and watched her subject closely. "I'm a detective with the Toronto police homicide squad."

Predictably, the color drained from Cheryl's face and the hand holding her coffee mug began to twitch ever so slightly.

"Hey, sis." The voice preceded the figure stepping into Cheryl's office.

Cheryl practically leaped out of her chair, sloshing coffee onto the carpeted floor. She set the messy mug down on the coffee table.

"Jumpy today?" He asked, his voice casual but his expression intent.

Cheryl took a deep breath and stiffened her shoulders as if to collect herself. "What is it, Andy?"

He was darkly good looking, like his sister. His eyes were nearly black, his dark hair slicked back. He was tall and trim, handsome in his Armani suit and shiny oxfords. His mannerisms were polished, like Cheryl's, but there was something far less innocent about him.

He shrugged, nodded politely at Stevie. "I noticed you have a visitor and wondered if I could be of any help."

Cheryl strode briskly to him. "Thank you, but I don't think there's anything you can do for us." She ushered him back to the door, her behavior bordering on rude. He shot another glance at Stevie before Cheryl soundly shut the door behind him.

Still pale and drawn looking, she returned to Stevie. She was distracted, unfocused, as she shakily picked up her mug and took a sip. "I'm sorry, Detective. My, ah, brother can be a bit overbearing at times." She laughed nervously again.

"No problem," Stevie answered, knowing Andrew Zachary Myatt was indeed a problem. Cheryl hadn't introduced them, a miscue the well-mannered woman wouldn't normally do, Stevie guessed. It told Stevie that Cheryl knew damn well what Stevie was here for. And that she didn't want her brother to know.

"Cheryl, I believe you have a close relationship with a suspect in a murder case I'm investigating."

Cheryl blinked hard, mentally grasping at her elusive composure.

Stevie, hands clasped in front of her, spoke quietly but firmly. "Vanessa Hedley has been questioned in connection with the death of her husband, James. She is a suspect in his murder, Cheryl." Stevie let the gravity of her words take root. "I have reason to believe that you might be able to verify her whereabouts on the night in question."

Cheryl brought a hand up to her mouth, then to her forehead, where it brushed a stray curl away. She made a grab for her coffee cup and clutched it for all she was worth.

"I, I'm sorry, I don't know what you're saying."

Stevie leaned forward, her voice gentle, almost soothing. She felt a twitch of regret at having to out this woman, to collapse her house of cards. The protective wall Cheryl Myatt had built around herself was quickly evaporating, thanks to Stevie. "I know you and Vanessa are lovers. I need to know if you spent the night with her last Friday night."

A corner of Cheryl's mouth began to twitch uncontrollably, her gaze faltering from Stevie's. She didn't answer — couldn't, it seemed — as her eyes began to fill with tears. A delicate hand rose to shield her tears from Stevie.

"Shit. I'm sorry."

"It's okay," Stevie said. "Take your time."

Stevie noticed a box of Kleenex on an end table and handed it to Cheryl. She waited for the tears to subside, giving her all the time she needed. Stevie needed this woman's help, needed her to be strong.

"Cheryl, believe me, I know this isn't easy. If there was any way I could have left you out of this, I would have. But I think you're an integral part of this case, and I'm sure you want to help Vanessa."

Cheryl nodded through her tears. "Of course I don't want her to go to jail for something she didn't do. She was the one who insisted on not telling anyone that we were together that night." She looked up at Stevie and asked in a quivering voice, "How did you find out?"

Stevie decided to do something she rarely ever did on the job — out herself. "My girlfriend is — or at least was at one time — a very good friend of Vanessa. Vanessa confided in her."

"I don't understand," Cheryl said, shaking her head. "Vanessa was so adamant about protecting me."

"Please, don't be upset with her or Jade. I'm sure the stress of it all was making Vanessa crazy and she needed to talk to someone about it. And Jade doesn't want to see Vanessa go to jail, so she told me."

Cheryl nodded slowly and swallowed the last of her tears. She straightened in her seat, her hands balling into fists. "I'll help you anyway I can. But I really don't want the press knowing anything about this."

"Of course," Stevie answered. "If it comes to trial, it will be public record. But until then, I'm certainly not going to tell anyone."

98

"Good." Cheryl breathed a sigh of relief. "I can't have them know about this right now."

"Your family?" Stevie prodded.

Cheryl nodded somberly. "Until Vanessa came along, my family was everything to me. I care very deeply for them and I don't want to hurt them. You see" — Cheryl faltered — "they really don't believe homosexuality is morally right. They are absolutely opposed to it. I mean, they've built a career around such beliefs." She spread her hands to include the whole room. "My father wants to be prime minister some day, probably my brother too, for that matter. If they found out about me —" She bit off her words, let them hang in the air. She looked devastated.

"Do they have any idea about you and Vanessa?"

"My brother saw us once, just having lunch together at a restaurant, for god's sake." She shook her head, anger rising in her voice. "I swear he had her investigated, because a couple of weeks later he came to me and warned me off her."

"Warned you off her?" Stevie repeated.

"Told me she'd had lesbian affairs in the past and that if I was seen with her, it would give people the wrong impression. Of course, I told him there was nothing to worry about. I told him I would not associate with her. That's why we've been so careful ever since."

"Did your brother ever threaten you in any way?"

Cheryl swatted dismissively at the air. "No, no. But I know damned well that I would be immediately cut off from the family. They would disown me. And I'd be quietly blacklisted in this city. My father has a lot of connections."

Stevie, who was estranged from her own family, couldn't imagine being disowned would be any worse than being so closeted. The distance from her family had only made her stronger, allowed her to blossom. But it wasn't her job to judge Cheryl Myatt or to reprimand her for the way she lived her life. "So you were with Vanessa the night her husband died?"

Cheryl stared at her hands, intertwined in her lap. "Yes." She looked up at Stevie. "We stayed at the Royal York that night under assumed names. We'd do that a couple of times a month so we could spend some time together."

"And the hotel staff will verify that for me?"

Cheryl looked hurt by Stevie's skepticism. "Of course. The one thing I wanted to hide from people, you already know about."

What Stevie really wanted to ask Cheryl was far too personal: Why the hell did this woman want anything to do with Vanessa Hedley? After the way she'd treated Jade years ago, and probably countless other lovers. And yet it was obvious Cheryl and Vanessa loved each other.

"Do you know anything about the kind of relationship Vanessa had with her husband?"

Cheryl shrugged. "I never met the man. But Vanessa told me she had never really loved him, that she'd dropped out of medical school and married him because he was ambitious and had money. She didn't talk about him much."

"Do you have any idea why she stayed with him?"

Cheryl sighed. "I really don't think she cared about the money any more. She told me she wanted to leave him. But it was because of me she stayed with him these last few months.

Stevie looked puzzled, her forehead creasing. "That's not quite the answer I was expecting."

Cheryl smiled. "Oh, we want to be together. Some day. But not now, not with my family considerations. Vanessa was happy to keep our little secret for now. She said she didn't trust her husband. If he knew about us, she figured he do something to give us a hard time."

Too late, Stevie thought. He knew about them all right, and was blackmailing *someone*. His company was on the downturn; he needed money. Like a vulture, he saw his opportunity and swooped in for the kill, only he was the one who'd fallen prey.

Stevie clapped her notebook shut. She hated what she had to do next. "Cheryl, there's something you need to be aware of. But I must warn you," Stevie said as she unclasped her briefcase, "this is part of a homicide investigation and you must not tell anyone about this."

Cheryl nodded gravely, her hands shaking again.

Stevie removed the photographs she'd found in Hedley's office and handed them to Cheryl. For a few seconds, Cheryl looked at them as though they were foreign objects that meant nothing to her. Then it dawned on her and her face collapsed.

"Oh my god," she whispered, her hand over her mouth, her eyes wide with stark fear. "Where did these come from?"

Stevie wouldn't give her the details, but told her they were in James Hedley's possession at the time of his death.

"Cheryl, do you have any idea who James Hedley might have been trying to blackmail with these photos?"

Cheryl shook her head, tears streaming down her face, her mascara running in streaks for what seemed like the hundredth time since their interview began. She reached for another Kleenex and blew her nose.

"Could it have been your father or your brother?"

Cheryl looked horrified. "Oh god. What are you saying, that Hedley was blackmailing them and they killed him or something?"

"No, no," Stevie soothed. "I'm not saying that at all. But I need to find out if he'd had a chance to contact any one about these or make any attempts at blackmail before he was killed."

Cheryl took a deep breath. "Look, if my family had been shown photos of Vanessa and me, I know they would have confronted me with it. Shit, they'd have gone ballistic on me."

"You're sure they wouldn't have kept it from you?"

"Positive. I know my family, Stevie."

CHAPTER NINE

It was Friday afternoon, and Stevie should have been glad it was the weekend. But there was so much work to do on this case, she could hardly see herself relaxing for the next two days. She knew what she really should do is insist on taking Jade and Tonka out to the country somewhere and renting a cabin for the weekend. But Stevie also knew it would never happen. She'd be like a caged animal until this case was solved.

Stevie and Jovanowski had spent a good portion of the morning updating their inspector on the case. The party witnesses had all been interviewed by Jovanowski, and he was delighted with the bombshell he'd been able to deliver. Three of the witnesses, who had stayed at Hedley's party until the bitter end, remembered seeing a woman in a blond wig and wearing an ugly blue dress show up late, seemingly out of nowhere. Those who were left at the party, including James Hedley, were so blitzed on booze and drugs that no one seemed to care who she was or whether she'd been invited. But Jovanowski had saved the best for last for Stevie and Inspector Jack McLemore. Two of the witnesses were sure the stranger, whom they remembered as slim and not particularly tall, was a transvestite.

McLemore had said warily, "And this didn't strike anyone at the party as weird, to have a transvestite, who nobody knows from Adam — or Eve — just show up suddenly?"

Jovanowski then explained that it was often an unlikely menagerie of people at James Hedley's parties. Some were coworkers, some were people he partied with at his favorite bar, usually a couple of hookers attended, sometimes his drug connection. The eclectic and unpredictable nature of his parties was a source of pride to Hedley, Stevie and Jovanowski had been told.

"At least that explains who the neighbor, Beatrice Robinson, saw leaving the house at about four in the morning," Stevie had noted at the meeting. "Now how in the hell we find this person, God only knows. I guess all we can do is a second round of interviews with the partygoers." Stevie shook her head in exasperation. "Roger Lemming will be the first on my list come Monday. First he doesn't tell me he'd had an affair with Vanessa, and then he forgets to mention this transvestite."

Jovanowski had laughed. "Tex, these witnesses are a joke. By the time some defense attorney gets through listing how many drinks and how many tokes they all had by the time our mystery transvestite showed up, the jury will figure they were all in the land of Oz."

They all agreed the transvestite angle was an interesting find, but until they came up with evidence of her presence and some kind of identity, it was of little use. In the meantime, they would concentrate their efforts on the motive and hope it would lead them back to the anonymous transvestite, who, Stevie and Jovanowski were sure, was their killer.

Alone together in the homicide squad conference room, Stevie and Jovanowski ate tasteless sandwiches brought in from the cafeteria while they pored over identical copies of a report they'd just received from the scenes of crime department.

Stevie laughed out loud.

"What?" Jovanowski peered at her from over his reading glasses.

"I was just picturing Andrew Myatt dressed as a woman." Stevie shook her head, amused. "Maybe he goes for that sort of thing, never know. Wouldn't that shock the hell out of the family."

"Is he short and thin?" Jovanowski asked sharply.

"Slim, but he's over six feet."

"Then it ain't him," Jovanowski barked.

"Sheesh, I'm only kidding around," Stevie mumbled, flipping another page.

"Jesus Christ!" Jovanowski blurted out, leaping up as though he'd just sat on hot coals.

"What is it?"

Jovanowski pitched his pencil against the far wall, his face reddening, the veins of his neck popping like popcorn kernels. "Goddamn idiots!"

"Who?" Stevie asked tersely, wishing he'd just spit it out.

"Our wonderful scenes of crime people. Take a look at page nineteen."

Stevie, who hadn't gotten that far in the report yet, flipped ahead and quickly scanned the page. Her stomach knotted at what Jovanowski was so incensed about. She rubbed her temple like it was a worry stone.

"Great, just great," she sighed. "They found an empty syringe under the floor mat of Vanessa's car. Analysis found traces of cocaine and heroin in it. No prints. Fuck."

"Fuck is right," Jovanowski yelled. "I knew I should have searched the car with them at the house, after you'd gone to the morgue. But I wanted to get a start on canvassing the neighborhood." Jovanowski paced. "Christ, why couldn't they have told us they found this thing earlier? They're gonna catch holy hell over this," he glared menacingly, pumping his fist in the air. "I'm gonna go throttle someone over this."

Stevie grabbed his wrist. "Just calm down, Ted. We'll go through the chain of command on this later." Stevie glanced at her watch. "Fortunately, Vanessa and her lawyer are due here in an hour, so we can ask her what she was doing with this needle. And we'd better get through this report by then in case there are any more surprises for us."

Jovanowski reluctantly sat down, sighing heavily, still breathing hard. "How'd you ever get her and that

Nazi lawyer to agree to another interview?" He winked slyly. "Did you tell them we know all about Vanessa doin' the funky thing with Cheryl Myatt?"

Stevie scowled at her partner. "I haven't told them anything, just that we have more evidence to discuss."

After her return earlier in the morning from interviewing Cheryl Myatt, Stevie admitted to Jovanowski how Jade had put her on to her. She'd selectively left out the part about Jade and Vanessa having been lovers once and simply told him they were college friends.

"Now here's something," Stevie said excitedly, her attention back on the report. "Page twenty-one. A strand of blond hair found in the master bed —"

"There were lots of blond hairs in the bedroom," Jovanowski interrupted. "Probably Vanessa's, if she'd ever decide to cooperate and allow us to take some of her hair to compare it with."

"No, look," Stevie continued. "It's a synthetic strand. From a wig."

Jovanowski shook his head slowly, a wan smile on his face. "Gotta hand it to our SOCO boys after all. They're pretty damned good."

"Yeah," Stevie chimed in. "But their communication skills sure suck."

Laura Redgrave sat rigidly across the table from Stevie and Jovanowski, her client a carbon copy beside her. Not much, not even pleasantries, had been exchanged so far, but Stevie detected a far more subdued — almost defeated — air about Vanessa Hedley this time.

Her lawyer, on the other hand, had her usual combative composure about her and was dressed — not surprisingly to Stevie — all in black. Only a white cravat peeked through, and Stevie, smiling to herself, devilishly fantasized about signing the woman up to a Marilyn Manson fan club.

"This had better be good, detectives," Redgrave warned, her voice low and ominous like distant thunder.

Stevie, smug in knowing she and Jovanowski had far more in their arsenal than at the last interview, nodded crisply. She let the lawyer sweat it out for a minute as she shuffled papers, stalling.

"Your client," Stevie finally said, nodding at Vanessa, "has insisted on offering us no alibi whatsoever. However, we have since learned of her whereabouts one week ago tonight."

Vanessa's shoulders slumped ever so slightly. She shot a nervous glance at her lawyer, who, as usual, was nonplussed. Vanessa looked back at Stevie, her face slowly coloring as she mentally made the link between Stevie and Jade. Her eyebrows quirked slightly, her chin lifting in acknowledgment. "I see you're well connected, Detective Houston."

Stevie grinned. "*Very* well connected."

"Anyways," Jovanowski cut in, oblivious to the subtle sparring match before him. "We know now that you were with Cheryl Myatt. She has verified this for us. We know that the two of you checked into the Royal York hotel last Friday night under assumed names. Hotel staff confirmed this for us this morning."

Vanessa's face hardened. Her eyes narrowed to

slits. She shook a finger in Stevie and Jovanowski's direction. "I do not want Cheryl Myatt brought into this mess. Is that understood?"

Stevie stared back, unblinking. "I'm afraid she's already a part of this. If she hadn't cooperated with us, you'd probably be arres —"

A fist thumped down on the table, drowning out Stevie's sentence. Vanessa was shaking, the red in her face splotchy in an abstract design. "You don't understand," she slowly enunciated. "If this gets out, I'll simply confess to murdering my husband."

Stevie leaned over the table on her elbows, everything about her demeanor uncompromising. She would not be cowed. "You do that and we proceed with a competency hearing."

"Look," Laura Redgrave cut in, her hand lightly clasping Vanessa's forearm. "Let's all just calm down here. If you two do your jobs and find the real killer, there won't be any need to justify Vanessa's whereabouts in a court of law."

Stevie and Jovanowski frowned in unison at the lawyer's barb.

Redgrave spoke again. "My client has an alibi, so we really don't have much to talk about right now, do we?"

"Not so fast," Stevie countered. "Our forensic experts have finished processing the scene and analyzing evidence. One of the things they found was a blond hair from a wig. Do you own a blond wig, Vanessa?"

Vanessa quickly shook her head. She seemed to have calmed down. "No, no. But that's not to say one of his girlfriends didn't."

Jovanowski took a pack of cough drops from his

shirt pocket and popped one in his mouth. It would never occur to him to offer one to anyone else. "Did he bring women back to the house often?"

Vanessa shrugged. "When I was out of town, yes. When he had these parties, I'm sure it was typical for him to get laid."

Stevie still marveled at how apathetic Vanessa Hedley was about her marriage, about her husband. Obviously, the marriage had been a joke, but Vanessa's callous attitude made her seem cold, hateful even. Cold and hateful enough to plot a murder and carry it out? Obsessed enough with her relationship with Cheryl and Cheryl's closeted lifestyle to kill her blackmailing husband? Stevie couldn't say if Vanessa had it in her to be a killer. She'd seen cases of upstanding, intelligent people who'd become cold-blooded killers for all sorts of reasons. Yes, Vanessa had played games with the detectives and yes, she was a first-class bitch. But was she the murderer of James Hedley? Stevie doubted it. On the contrary, Stevie felt Vanessa may well be a victim. Someone, it seemed, was trying to set her up.

"There is another piece of physical evidence," Jovanowski said almost anticlimactically. "A syringe was found under a floor mat in your car, Vanessa. There were traces of cocaine and heroin in the needle, which is believed to be the cause of your husband's overdose."

They watched Vanessa's hand begin shaking uncontrollably, an eye twitching in sync. Her lawyer furiously whispered in her ear.

Laura Redgrave spoke next. "And were my client's prints on the needle?"

Jovanowski cleared his throat, the cough drop tinkling against his molars. "No prints."

"Detectives, I would like a moment alone with my client."

"Of course," Stevie answered, rising.

In the hallway, Jovanowski paced. "I think she did it."

Stevie leaned against the wall, arms folded over her chest. Laying their opinions on the table always helped them navigate the twists and turns of a case. "You do?"

Jovanowski stopped his pacing and spread his beefy hands in exasperation. "Look, she's got a motive, or several motives as a matter of fact. She inherits a big wad of dough, she gets the scumbag out of her life. *And*, if she knew about this blackmailing thing, then killing Hedley puts a stop to that so little girlie-girl's family doesn't have to find out about them."

"There were lots of people who could have had motives to kill James Hedley, from what we know of him," Stevie shot back. "It could have been a drug debt gone bad, a business deal that soured, some woman's jealous husband. Christ, I don't know. But I don't think it was Vanessa. If she's that protective of Cheryl Myatt, she wouldn't risk murdering dear hubby over it."

"Nah." Jovanowski shook his head. "Being so protective of Cheryl Myatt is exactly why she'd off that little bastard. He was about to blow their affair wide open unless he got a nice payoff. And who knows, even then he might have decided to spill the beans just to be a miserable prick. I don't think Vanessa wanted to take that chance."

"I think we're reaching here, Ted."

Jovanowski resumed his pacing, making Stevie feel like she was on a merry-go-round. "There were no signs of break and enter at the house, so —"

"Yeah," Stevie interrupted. "And there was a party, which usually means people are invited into the house."

Jovanowski sighed. "Still though, she's the first one to find the body, like wasn't that convenient. And then we find a needle in her car."

"A needle with no prints," Stevie reminded him.

Jovanowski shrugged. "So she probably wore rubber gloves." He stopped and looked at Stevie. "Is Jade sure about the time of death being between four and six in the morning?"

Stevie shoved her hands into her pants pocket. "I'm going to see her this afternoon. She left me a voice mail saying the final autopsy report's in. And yeah, she's pretty sure about time of death."

Jovanowski crossed an arm over his wide chest and cupped his double chin with his other hand. Heavy graying eyebrows shadowed his eyes. "So maybe Vanessa slipped out of the hotel unseen between four and six, or maybe the girlfriend is covering for her being there all night."

"Ted, everything we have is still circumstantial. All Vanessa has to do is have some witnesses tell the jury what a shithead her husband was, how tons of people hated him. Then she can take the stand herself, bat her eyelashes, and tell the court how used and abused she was and how she's being victimized all over again by being charged with his murder. And charged by a homophobic cop and a jealous cop, no less."

"Well, since *you're* gay, you're saying I'm the homophobic one?" Jovanowski asked, looking hurt. "And what are you jealous of?"

Stevie sighed. "Never mind, it's a long story."

"Christ, I wish I could have a smoke right now," Jovanowski grumbled.

"Vanessa probably does too."

"Why are you defending her all of a sudden anyway? Earlier in the week you couldn't stand the sight of her."

Stevie shrugged. "I just don't think it's our job to take these half-assed hypotheses of ours to court and dump them in some jury's lap." She looked squarely at her partner. "I don't want to stop this investigation until we find out who really killed James Hedley. Even if it means weeks of tracking down every person who could possibly have had a motive to kill him."

Laura Redgrave popped her head out the door. "We're ready in here."

Redgrave informed Stevie and Jovanowski that her client, albeit reluctantly, would now tell them everything she knew. True to her word, Vanessa told them she and Cheryl Myatt had begun their affair nine months ago and that she'd wanted to leave her husband, but Cheryl was afraid of creating waves. So they'd settled for weekly trysts in hotel rooms, the back seats of a cars, wherever they could grab a few minutes alone. And no, she had no idea where the needle in her car had come from — it wasn't hers.

Stevie drummed her fingers on the tabletop. "Did you notice anyone following you to the Royal York that night, or home the next morning?"

Vanessa shook her head.

"Did you park in a public parking lot at the hotel?" Stevie asked.

"Of course." Vanessa swallowed visibly, and a tear began to slither down her heavily powdered cheek. Her voice cracked. "At first I thought it was just you people out to give me a hard time." She looked at both Stevie and Jovanowski, her eyes wide like a frightened child's. "Someone's out to get me. You think so too, don't you?"

Stevie glanced at Jovanowski, knowing there'd be disapproval on his face for what was coming next. "Yes, Vanessa, I do. We want to help you, and that's why we need you to help us."

Vanessa nodded, lips pursed.

"There's something else," Stevie said darkly. She pulled the photos from her briefcase and slid them across the table.

Shock, the same sort of shock and hurt Stevie had seen yesterday on Cheryl Myatt's face, now played across Vanessa's face. She pressed a well-manicured hand to her lips. "My god," she choked.

"I take it you didn't know about these," Jovanowski said gruffly.

Vanessa shook her head, as though words were too much effort. She cleared her throat, took a couple of deep breaths.

"Could someone have been blackmailing your husband?" Stevie asked.

Vanessa let out a laugh that had no joy in it. "Well, if they were, James wouldn't have given a shit. He wouldn't have paid out a single dime to keep my affair with Cheryl under wraps."

"Do you have any idea who he was blackmailing, then?"

Vanessa focused on the ceiling. "That bastard!" She absently played tug of war with a Kleenex between her fingers, shaking her head slowly, more tears spilling down her cheeks. "Christ, I don't know. If it was money he was after, then I guess it was someone with money." She thought for a moment, and her eyes widened with a new realization. "God, I hope he wasn't trying to blackmail Cheryl's family."

Stevie and Jovanowski shared a glance. It was Stevie who answered. "That's what we're trying to find out."

Jade munched her granola bar, washing it down with coffee. The granola and the apple she'd just eaten had been lunch. Two autopsies had consumed her morning, and paperwork had totally eaten up her lunch hour. No chance of her starting the weekend early.

A knock on her door interrupted Jade's self-pity.

"Come in," she called out flatly.

"Hi, honey."

It was Stevie, and they embraced, Jade burrowing into the strong arms of her lover.

"Mmm, this feel's wonderful," Jade exulted into Stevie's shoulder, feeling her mood soar for the first time all day.

"Rough day, hon?"

Jade broke away, nodded grimly, and ran her

fingers through her jet-black hair. She was approaching forty and still no signs of gray, which pissed Stevie off to no end. At six years younger, Stevie had recently begun to notice a few strands of gray infiltrating her brown hair.

"How about you, how's your day going?" Jade asked, moving back to the well-worn chair behind her desk.

Stevie sighed grumpily. "Our SOCO people found a syringe in Vanessa's car at the house last Saturday."

"And they're just telling you now?"

Stevie nodded, frowning, and plunked down in the old wood chair across from Jade. "Had traces of coke and heroin in it. No prints on it, of course."

Jade whistled. "Wow. That certainly makes things interesting. Still think whoever Hedley was blackmailing is responsible for this, or is Vanessa still at the top of your list?"

Stevie shrugged. "She's still at the top of Ted's list. Me, I think she's being set up."

Jade twirled her pen between her fingers like it was a marching band baton. "I think your instinct on this is right on, and not because I know Vanessa."

"Well, I figure Hedley had it coming to him. Oops," Stevie laughed in jest, winking. "I'm not supposed to say things like that, am I?"

Jade laughed too. "Darling, too late to try and hide your cynicism from me now. I know you're a crusty cop."

Stevie squinted at the granola wrapper on Jade's desk, her face twisting into a grimace. "Geez, you always have to eat so goddamned healthy. You got any cookies in that desk?"

Jade smiled. That was her Stevie, the incorrigible

sweet tooth. "No, no cookies. Sorry. Hey, listen, do you think Vanessa's in any danger?"

Stevie spread her hands out in frustration. "I told her she shouldn't be staying alone in that house. She should either have someone stay with her or go to a motel and register under an assumed name. I don't think she appreciated the advice. She's pretty damn headstrong."

Jade shook her head slowly, a wisp of a smile on her lips. "That she is, but you're just as bad. You interviewed her today?"

Stevie nodded. "She's only too happy to cooperate now that we already know about her relationship with Cheryl Myatt. I guess she's finally figured out that so long as she's not the one on trial, the relationship shouldn't have to become public."

Jade reached into her bottom drawer and pulled out an inch-thick report. "James Hedley's autopsy report." She slid it across her desk to Stevie.

"And?" Stevie asked, brown eyes already zeroed in on the report.

"Just as I thought." Jade took a sip of her now lukewarm coffee. "A lethal combination of coke and heroin. Enough to kill a horse, actually."

"So no chance with that amount that it was just recreational?"

"No way," Jade agreed. "Some drug users will inject a combination of the two; it's known as speedballing. But not with those amounts. The guy didn't have a chance."

Lips pursed, Stevie tucked the report into her briefcase. "Guess I've got my bedtime reading for tonight."

Jade came around the desk and sat on Stevie's

knee, wrapping her arms around her lover's neck. "I was kind of hoping I could find some other bedtime activity for us tonight." She kissed Stevie on the mouth, her body tingling from the memory of their making up.

Stevie caressed Jade's cheek and winked seductively. "You just might be able to talk me into something."

Jade grinned. "Talking won't be necessary."

They kissed again until Stevie's hand began crawling up Jade's thigh. Jade leapt up like she'd been poked with a cattle prod. "Oh no you don't."

"Why not?" Stevie sulked. "Now's as good a time as any." She lowered her voice, her eyes half slits. "It's one way to clear your desk off, honey."

Jade wagged her finger at Stevie, a big grin sapping any real intent from the scolding she was about to deliver. "Stephanie Houston, we both have work to do, and this is not helping us get it done."

Stevie stood up and saluted. "Yes, ma'am."

"Where are you off to now?"

"Back to the office. More phone calls to make. I need to set up an interview with Andrew Myatt, and I still need to see Roger Lemming again." Stevie shook her head in exasperation. "He keeps conveniently forgetting to tell me things."

"Are you working on this case all weekend?"

Stevie shrugged a what-can-I-do.

"Maybe I can help you."

Stevie smiled and picked up her briefcase. "I'll take help wherever I can get it." At the door she spun around as if she'd just remembered something. "I hope your strange little assistant hasn't been starting any more fires around here."

Jade sighed heavily and rolled her eyes. "I think he's learned his lesson."

"See you at home tonight, hon." Stevie blew a kiss to Jade.

CHAPTER TEN

Stevie, glancing at her watch again, knocked on the closed door of the constituency office of Member of Parliament John Myatt. It wasn't exactly what she wanted to be doing on a Saturday morning. Sleeping in with Jade, Tonka curled up on the floor beside the bed, the automatic coffee maker sending wafts of fresh coffee aroma drifting upstairs — now *that* would be an ideal Saturday morning.

Stevie moaned quietly for what wasn't, and took small pleasure in the fact that Secretary Bitch wouldn't be here. She wasn't in the mood for nosy, judgmental, and downright unpleasant people. Though she had to admit to herself, when *was* she in the mood for people like that?

The door opened and Andrew Myatt, all six-feet, three inches of him, Stevie instantly calculated, stood with a threadlike smile on his face, square chin jutting out in mild defiance. Or perhaps it was bravado — Stevie couldn't be sure. He looked trim and fit in gray cotton chinos and a dark red Ralph Lauren polo shirt. His gelled black hair, just as it had the last time, resembled a plastic helmet — not a strand out of place.

They shook hands — hers firm and professional, his cold and dry.

"Please, come in," he said, his voice like a cold rain.

"Thank you for meeting me here on a Saturday," Stevie replied, stepping into the plush carpeted office. The room was even larger than Cheryl's office, but masculine in decor where hers had been feminine. The colors were all dark, the furniture chunky and overbearing, the wood heavy and ornate.

He sat behind his large oak desk and motioned for Stevie to sit across from him in one of the two leather wing chairs.

There would be no cozy discussion in front of the fireplace in *this* office. No fresh coffee brewing either.

"I'm quite used to working Saturdays." He looked at Stevie with eyes as dark as coal and with about as much emotion. His hands rested on the polished desktop, long fingers intertwined.

He had hands very much like his sister, Stevie thought. Feminine and slender.

"Now, what is it I can do for you, Officer Houston?" His tone was formal rather than helpful.

Stevie didn't bother correcting him on her title. "I'm afraid my business here won't be very pleasant." She took out her notepad, wrote down the date, time, and place. "Did you know a man by the name of James Hedley?"

Andrew Myatt cleared his throat and took his time answering. "Yes, I knew who he was. Though I didn't actually *know* him."

"When did you first become aware of him?"

"Well, I'd heard his name a couple of years ago. Read about his investment company in the newspaper or somewhere." Myatt frowned. "He wasn't a contributor to the party or to my father's campaigns, so there really was no need for me to go out of my way to get to know him."

What a guy, Stevie thought, wishing she could give in to the urge to roll her eyes. Unless you could do something for the Myatts or their party, you were of no use. "I take it that at some point you spoke to him or met him?"

Myatt's hands were gripped together so tightly his knuckles had begun to blanch. A fine bead of sweat popped out on his low hairline. Suddenly aware of his hands, he slid them under the desk and out of view. He cleared his throat again. "He telephoned me about a month ago. Asked me to meet him."

Stevie's eyebrows shot up. She knew it was about the photos. "And?"

Myatt sat stock-still, barely breathing, it seemed to Stevie. Even his mouth hardly moved when he talked, his eyes empty and unblinking. "So I did. I met the fat little prick," he spat, his tone venemous.

"What did he want?"

Myatt shrugged with one eyebrow, his voice calm again. "Wanted to show me some pictures of my sister and his lovely wife."

Stevie popped open her briefcase and removed the well-traveled photos. She piled them neatly on the desk.

Myatt shot a brief glance at the top photo. "That's them. Charming, aren't they?" he said mockingly. He shook his head, his mouth twisting into a bitter scowl. "Wanted me to pay a hundred and fifty thousand for the photos and the negatives. Said he'd take them to the media if I didn't."

"Did you pay him?"

Myatt's laugh was loud and hollow. "Are you kidding?"

"Did you already know your sister was a lesbian, Mr. Myatt?" Stevie asked, almost pleased to see someone so far on the political right have to confront homosexuality in such a personal way. It was easy for people like the Myatts to cast stones at others, at outsiders.

Myatt stared hard at Stevie, his face set like concrete. It seemed an eternity before he spoke, his voice razor sharp. "My sister is not a lesbian. This" — he pointed accusingly at Vanessa in the top photo — "*slut* may be, but Cheryl is normal."

Stevie felt herself stiffen at his choice of words. If there was anyone connected to this case who was not normal, Andrew Myatt would be her first choice. She couldn't help but engage, just a little. "What makes you say your sister is not gay when clearly she is seen here making love with another woman. A woman, I might add, who is a murder suspect."

Myatt's face began to flush. "I don't know what the hell that woman did to my sister, but I can assure you, Cheryl would not have done this willingly."

Stevie knew it would be easy to become embroiled in an argument with Myatt, but she knew it would solve nothing. He would have to deal with his sister's lifestyle in his own twisted way.

"I do know, Mr. Myatt, that your sister does not want to hurt your family. In fact, it's for that reason that she has been sneaking around with Vanessa Hedley. As you can see, her secret has left her vulnerable to blackmail."

For just a flash, Stevie thought she saw a pained expression sweep across Myatt's face.

He ran his hand nervously over his freshly shaved chin, his eyes intent on a glass paperweight on his desk. "It's potentially a time bomb that could seriously hurt this family politically. It could be devastating," he said quietly but unequivocally.

Stevie tapped her pen softly on her notepad. "Then why not pay James Hedley what he wanted?"

Myatt shook his head and looked at Stevie. "You can't win at those games. People like . . . *him* . . . are despicable. You pay him now, and two months later he's after you again for more." Myatt's hands returned to the desk, clenched into fists. "You cannot let people like *that* have any control over you. They get you by the balls once, and they've got you for good."

Stevie could feel the sting of Andrew Myatt's simmering rage again. He was a man brimming with anger. "So you told Hedley to get lost?"

"Damn right I did. Told him to shove those pictures up his ass."

"And what about your sister? How will you protect

your family's political name if her lifestyle becomes public? You should know there is a chance that should this case go to trial, your sister's relationship with Vanessa Hedley may be entered into the record."

Myatt sat back in his chair, his hands now quietly in his lap. He smirked. "I will not let my sister hurt this family," he said slowly and evenly. "If need be, she will be cut loose and we shall publicly condemn her lifestyle." He shrugged as though he sensed Stevie's disapproval. "I mean, we simply can't condone this. It would be the death of us."

Stevie rubbed her right temple, not surprised by Andrew Myatt's ruthlessness, but disgusted nevertheless. "Did you know your sister was with Vanessa Hedley the night James Hedley was murdered?"

Myatt cleared his throat, coughed once. "No, I was not aware of that."

"Were you still having her followed as of last weekend?"

They stared at each other for a long time, as if in some kind of duel, until Myatt finally blinked. His tone was searing. "No, I was not still having my sister followed."

Stevie leaned forward, elbows resting on her knees. "Where were you last Friday night, Mr. Myatt?"

He looked stunned that Stevie would be asking him for an alibi. His mouth opened, then closed abruptly until he finally composed himself enough to talk. "I was home with my wife. We went to bed early."

Stevie stood up. "You were home all night?"

Myatt stood too, crossing his arms over his chest as if to ward off Stevie's suspicions. "Of course I was home all night."

He followed her to the door. "I tried to warn my sister about her, you know."

Stevie turned around. "About Vanessa?"

Myatt nodded, chin defiant again. "I could tell she was nothing but trouble. At least if she goes to jail, she won't be able to bother my sister any more."

Stevie left the building with Myatt's parting words swirling in her mind, chilling her along with the cool September air. Could he have wanted both James and Vanessa Hedley out of his life bad enough to have one killed and the other set up to look like the murderer?

Stevie pulled into the driveway of the small brick Scarborough bungalow, parking behind Roger Lemming's silver BMW sedan. The car looked pretentiously out of place beside such a plain, middle-class house, Stevie thought as she walked up the chipped cement walk. The car didn't surprise her in the least. Lemming seemed to like the finer things in life; champagne tastes on cold duck salary.

She'd gotten Lemming's home address from his criminal record in the Toronto police computer system. It was time to let the hammer fall on him. Time to extract some answers from him, for Stevie was sure he knew more than he'd let on.

She rapped firmly on the front door and tried to ignore her growling stomach. It was noon already, and the piece of toast she'd scarfed down for breakfast just wasn't cutting it.

Stevie hardly recognized Lemming when he opened the door. There was two days' growth of beard on his face, his blond hair was unwashed and disheveled, and his clothes resembled a bag of dirty laundry. He smelled of whiskey and stale cigarettes.

"Hello, Stevie," he slurred, her name sounding more like Sshtevie. His grin was lopsided. "Or is it Detective Houston today?"

"You can call me whatever you want, Roger. Can I come in?"

He staggered away from the door to let her pass. "C'mon in and have a drink with me."

Stevie glanced at the bottle of Seagram's in his hand, mildly surprised it wasn't something more expensive. Must save his good stuff for when he's trying to impress people, she thought. "I don't think so, Roger." She nodded at the bottle. "You've gotten an early start on the day, I see."

Lemming laughed as though it was the funniest thing he'd ever heard. "I'm not starting the day, babe. I'm finishing last night!"

He laughed again, wiped the tears from his cheeks, and followed Stevie into the cluttered living room that looked like it hadn't been vacuumed or dusted in a month.

Stevie brushed the fabric cushion of the couch before she sat down. She watched Lemming fall into the chair opposite her, the contents of the bottle sloshing onto his lap. She cursed under her breath. A drunken interview would be pretty much useless to her. He probably wouldn't remember whatever he told her, and even if he did, it would be easy for him to deny it and claim he was too drunk to know what he was saying.

"So." He leered at Stevie. "You come to talk to me about Vanessa again?"

"Well, actually —"

"She's pretty fucking hot in bed, that one. An animal." He winked slyly. "You'd never know she was into chicks."

Stevie clasped her hands in her lap, her Windbreaker still zipped up. There was no point in taking her notepad out — it would be nothing but a short fishing expedition. She smiled conspiratorially. "Did that turn you on?"

"What, that she liked chicks?" Lemming took a swig from his bottle, wiped his mouth with the back of his hand. He shrugged. "I don't know why she'd wanna suck pussy. Hell, I made her happy in the sack. Fucked her *real* good. Had her begging." He shook his head, bewilderment on his face. "I don't know why she'd need anything else, you know?"

No, I don't know. Stevie couldn't decide whether to laugh at Roger Lemming or feel sorry for him. He obviously saw himself as the ultimate sex machine, chock-full of desire, charm, looks, and the finer things in life. Everything a woman could ever want. *Yeah, right.*

"Roger, why didn't you tell me about the transvestite at Hedley's party? You had to have known she was there. It was late, and you and only a handful of others were there."

Lemming shrugged lazily. "So what. There were always lots of weirdos at his parties."

"Did you notice any unusual behavior from her? Did you have any idea who she was?"

Lemming laughed straight from his belly, his head rolling back. "You must be either really stupid or really innocent."

Stevie steeled her jaw, growing angrier by the minute at this loser. He obviously had no intention of helping her solve this case, for whatever perverse reason. Maybe he really just didn't give a shit.

"Look," he finally said. "All anybody at that party cared about was scoring a few lines and getting their rocks off, okay? I don't know about anythin' else that night."

Stevie decided to change the subject, giving Lemming one last chance to show his worth. "Roger, did you know James Hedley was blackmailing a man by the name of Andrew Myatt?"

Lemming stared at Stevie, his eyes not focusing on her. He took another gulp of whiskey. "I don't know what you're talkin' about."

Stevie rested her elbows on her knees and leaned forward. "The photos I showed you, remember? Vanessa and another woman having sex in the back of a car."

Lemming shrugged. "I don't give a fuck who Vanessa screws. Fucking bitch dumped me pretty fast. Guess I wasn't rich enough for her to wanna keep sucking my dick."

Stevie was stunned at the vitriol coming from Roger Lemming's mouth. She'd had no idea he harbored such hate for Vanessa. Quite a switch from her first interview with him, when he claimed he hardly knew Vanessa Hedley.

He wasn't finished his bitter tirade. "I bet this bitch Vanessa's banging is rich." He stared at the wall, hatred in his eyes. "She'd have to be. Vanessa doesn't do anything unless it's for money. I bet she even killed that fat bastard of a husband of hers just to get some money from his will or whatever."

Stevie found herself fascinated by the dark side of Roger Lemming and his preoccupation with money and sex. She wondered if he actually cared about anyone else but himself. *Probably not.*

She got up.

"Leaving so soon? I can tell you more about what a bitch that Vanessa is." He staggered after Stevie. "She actually told me one time, right after I made her come, that she'd been in love once." He grinned.

Stevie felt her face warming and walked faster toward the door. She didn't want to hear this shit.

Lemming laughed. "She even told me it was a woman. From years ago. Said she didn't think she'd ever love anybody again, so she might as well have a good time fucking everything that moved." His laugh was acrimonious. "Hell, I don't believe that bitch. All she cares about is money."

"Bye, Roger." Stevie let the screen door slam behind her. She swallowed hard as she started her car and wished like hell she'd never met or heard of Vanessa Hedley. Or Roger Lemming.

She pulled out of the driveway, sure in her gut that she wasn't finished with Roger Lemming yet.

CHAPTER ELEVEN

Jade greeted Stevie at the door with a giant, soul-nurturing hug and an energetic kiss for all the neighborhood to see.

"Mmm. What'd I do to deserve that?" Stevie asked, stepping inside and shutting the heavy oak door. She dipped Jade à la Fred Astaire and Ginger Rogers and kissed her.

"I kissed you because you're special and you're mine," Jade whispered in Stevie's ear.

Stevie laughed as Jade righted herself. "We must make people gag when we act like that."

Jade shrugged, then wrapped her arms around Stevie's neck. "Frankly, I don't care if they choke. Let them, my sweet, because I have every intention of being as affectionate as I want."

"Believe me, I don't want you to stop."

"How'd your interview with Myatt go today?" Jade asked as she began nuzzling and kissing Stevie's neck.

Stevie threw her head back, enjoying the attention. "Pretty much what I expected. The guy's homophobic and doesn't have any use for Vanessa." Stevie groaned as Jade's kisses trailed down her throat. She kicked off her Nike runners. "Stopped in on Roger Lemming, too."

Jade looked up. "How'd that go?"

Stevie playfully pushed Jade's head back to her. "Don't stop, honey. And Lemming's a real nut, by the way. Hates Vanessa's guts."

"Mmm, that makes things interesting," Jade mumbled between soft kisses. "I think *you're* getting closer."

Stevie gasped as Jade began to release the buttons of her shirt. "And I think you're getting closer, my sweet."

Jade grinned and gently squeezed Stevie's breasts, backing her against the wall.

"Oh, baby, I love this new aggressive you," Stevie growled playfully. Her breathing turned ragged as she felt Jade's tongue trail down her cleavage.

The doorbell rang just as Stevie was about to pull Jade to the floor.

"Aw shit," Stevie groaned, struggling to do up her buttons. "Maybe we shouldn't answer it." She hastily tucked her shirt in.

Jade smiled her disappointment and said over

Tonka's barking, "Not with both our cars out front and Tonka barking her head off."

Jade opened the door to Tess, clad in black Levi's jeans and a yellow Nike jacket with her softball team's logo emblazoned on it. She shifted from sneaker to sneaker on the stoop.

"Hey. Bad time?"

Jade grinned naughtily as Stevie, behind her, raked her fingers through her short but tousled hair. "Actually, we were a little busy," Jade teased.

Tess began to blush and cast her eyes down in that endearingly bashful way of hers. "Sorry, guys," she mumbled. "I'll stop by later."

Stevie grabbed Tess by the wrist and yanked her in — no small feat considering Tess had a good inch and at least fifteen pounds on Stevie. "You'll do no such thing. We're just going to fix something for lunch before I starve to death."

Jade took Tess's jacket from her and threw it over the banister. "Can't promise it'll be gourmet, but come and join us."

Tess shrugged and nodded, following them into the kitchen. She said hello to Tonka and gave her an affectionate pat on the way.

"So, what's new, girl?" Stevie asked, pulling a loaf of bread from the bread box. From the fridge she retrieved a couple of bottles of beer, handing one to Tess, then grabbed a hunk of cheddar.

Tess twisted the cap off the bottle and pulled out a wicker stool from the kitchen's island. "Not much. Working tomorrow night."

Jade's eyebrows bobbed up and down. A slow grin spread across her face. "And what's on your plate tonight, hot stuff?"

Tess's face colored again as she gave that familiar aw-shucks shrug. She could be so shy at times, yet Stevie and Jade had seen her in action at the neighborhood dyke bar. Tess Hewitson was a chick magnet. The women seemed to love the combination of the gruff but shy exterior, the quiet intelligence, the sweet vulnerability Tess seemed to ooze. Tess was full of contradictions — the ultimate aphrodisiac, it seemed. Still, she acted as though she couldn't quite believe the stampede of women were after *her*.

"Nothin's on my plate tonight. Probably a video and a couple of beers.

Jade, helping Stevie with the grilled cheese sandwiches, shook her head at Tess, pretend scorn all over her face. "Girl, if you're going to meet the woman of your dreams, you can't be sitting at home alone on a Saturday night."

Tess sighed and swilled a mouthful of beer. "Trust me, I've had my share of one-night stands. I'm through test driving cars. I'm gonna wait for it to come to me."

"Well," Stevie said, carefully placing the sandwiches in the oven, "since you're off the market, how about watching a video with a couple of old married broads tonight?"

Tess laughed. "I'd love to. But do you have time, Stevie? Aren't you wrapped up with this case?"

Jade winked at Tess and hopped up on her knee. "Honey, if she's busy with that case tonight, you and I can watch the movie together."

"Not on your life!" Stevie said pointedly, wagging a metal spatula at them. She laughed heartily as Jade leaped off Tess as though she'd sat down on a hot stove.

Jade scurried to Stevie and kissed her. "Wouldn't dream of it, dear. Oh, and before I forget, Ted phoned this morning while you were out. He and Jocelyn have decided to take off for the weekend to patch things up."

Stevie opened the oven door to check on the sandwiches, which were browning nicely. "Good. I hope it works out or else he'll be miserable for the rest of his life."

"And," Jade continued, "I have some more news for you."

Stevie pulled the sandwiches from the oven and set them on plates. "What's that, love?"

"I spent some time on the Internet this morning. I looked up some articles on Andrew Myatt."

Stevie did a double take. "You did?" She joined Tess on a stool at the island.

Jade, a proud grin on her face, put her hand up. "Hang on a minute." She disappeared upstairs, then jogged down with a sheaf of papers in her hand. She tossed them on the counter in front of Stevie and pulled up a stool beside her.

Stevie set her half-eaten sandwich down, intent on reading the material. "You never cease to amaze me, hon." She shot a wink at Jade. "Maybe later tonight I'll even show how much you amaze me."

Tess cleared her throat to interrupt. "All right, you perpetual honeymooners. I can take a hint. I'll leave you guys to it tonight."

Stevie playfully jabbed Tess's arm. "Hey, don't worry about it. When you own the cow, you can get all the milk you want, whenever you want."

Jade, in turn, slapped Stevie's wrist. "Watch it, honey, or the cow might move on to another pasture."

Stevie's jaw dropped in a mock show of hurt. "What'd I say?"

"Anyway," Jade said to change the subject, "I've also talked to someone at the University of Toronto Library, where Myatt went to school in the early eighties. The back issues of the student newspaper are electronically filed now, so they're going to email me any articles they can find on him."

"Your old alma mater," Stevie said to Jade. "Did you ever hear of him when you were a student there?"

Jade shook her head and swallowed a mouthful of the now-cold cheese sandwich. "He was probably on the main campus if he was a poli sci major. The medical students were on a different campus."

Stevie returned her attention to the feature article in front of her, from *Vanity Fair* magazine last year. She read parts of it out loud. The article told how Andrew Myatt was a relentless worker on his father's behalf, the elder member of parliament's right-hand man. He had a reputation for being ruthless and calculating, possessing a piercing intelligence, and having a brisk manner in dealing with people. His family came first, the article said, and he was fiercely protective of his father's name and political career.

Stevie read from the article: "The seeds of the younger Myatt's conservative views were likely planted at a very young age — if not inherited from generations of right-wing activists — but his views became firmly ensconced in university, where he surrounded himself with like-minded thinkers and corresponding activities.

"One of those activities included conceptualizing and then spearheading a student activist group called the 'Moral Mercenaries.' The dubious nature of the group has remained somewhat mysterious over the years, with members sworn to secrecy. The group folded after just a few years, but at least one insider said the group's purpose was to call attention to so-called immoral activities in a very public and in the most shameful way possible. Their targets included liberal politicians, well-known union leaders, high profile social activists, and even a well-known Canadian male figure skater."

The article went on to say the Moral Mercenaries believed that by creating a moral crisis or the public shaming of a well-known individual, it provided fuel for the political right to convince voters that society was falling apart around them and that certain politicians — people like Andrew Myatt's father — could lead the masses to a more moral society.

By using subversive and highly secretive tactics, the group's members would out closeted homosexuals, expose infidelity scandals, and even set people up to be caught with a prostitute.

Of course, Andrew Myatt, in an interview with the article's author, denied he was heavily involved with the group and said he had had no idea what some of its members were up to.

Tess whistled. "Wow. Talk about low-class scumbags. I wouldn't even do that shit to my worst enemies, let alone people I didn't even know."

Stevie sipped her beer, then spoke quietly. "Well, my impression of Andrew Myatt is certainly correct."

"C'mon," Jade said, leaping off her stool. "Let's go upstairs to the computer and see if they've sent that stuff yet."

Stevie and Tess followed Jade upstairs to a spare bedroom that had been turned into an office. It was a large room, with polished wood floors and wall-to-ceiling bookshelves that were stocked to the brim. A desk as big as a table was the centerpiece of the room, and it sat atop a bright, circular Oriental rug. It was a far more impressive office than either Jade or Stevie possessed at work.

Jade fired up the computer and logged on. She clicked into the mail program and typed in her password. A familiar jingle indicated there was mail. She clicked on the message, which was from the University of Toronto, and read out loud that two articles had been found, both of which were attached.

Jade logged off the Net and clicked on the computer's attachment folder. The first article was only about five years old and talked about Myatt's accomplishments since graduating from the U of T. It was a positive story, and Jade noted from the date the article appeared around the university's annual alumni donation drive. The story was probably done with the hope that an appreciative Myatt would donate money to the university.

The next article had them all squinting at the screen, each silently reading. It was dated from 1982 and was a story on the Moral Mercenaries. It was a weak story, glossing over the group's real agenda. There was a photo of five men sitting together in a circle, and the caption indicated the five were the brain trust behind the group. Myatt was one of the men. Stevie's jaw dropped as she read the name Roger Lemming.

"Holy shit!" she yelled, her face suddenly ashen. "That son-of-a-bitch." She knew she should feel angry at Lemming for having lied to her so many times, but instead she felt a strange surge of panic. A sour taste had formed in her mouth.

"That's the same Roger Lemming you've been dealing with?" Jade asked in surprise.

Stevie studied the picture again and slapped the desk. "Goddamn it, that's him! I just asked him today if he knew James Hedley was blackmailing the Myatts, and he denied the whole thing. Acted like he'd never even heard of the Myatts. I'm going to go pay him a visit, and this time I'll haul him down to headquarters and see how he likes being interrogated all night long."

"Wait," Jade said quietly, studying the screen. "I know this other guy in the photo, this dweeb here." She pointed to a thin, dark-haired man with a full beard and longish hair. His glasses were as thick as Coke bottles.

"Who is it?" Stevie asked.

Jade shook her head as though remembering something unpleasant. "Charles Fleming. He was in med school with Vanessa and me. He dropped out in third year, not long after Vanessa."

Tess said, "I can see you weren't a fan of his."

Jade rolled her eyes. "I thought he was a nut case. Doesn't surprise me that he belonged to that group. He seemed pretty weird."

"How so?" Stevie asked.

Jade shrugged. "He never really talked to anybody, just kept to himself. But I always had the strange feeling that he was watching me. Vanessa, too."

Stevie felt a twinge of alarm. "What do you mean watching you?"

Jade struggled to remember. "It's hard to put your

finger on it, but he just seemed to be, like, skulking around, watching us when we were together. Almost like he knew about us. In fact he'd had a crush on Vanessa in first year, I remember. Kept asking her out, sending flowers, stuff like that."

"Did she ever go out with him?"

Jade shook her head. "No way. He was way too weird. He definitely had a thing for her, though. Then I think he sensed, or maybe saw something in Vanessa and me when we were together, but I swear he *knew* we were an item, even though we were being discreet. It wasn't long after that that Vanessa started getting hateful notes and phone calls."

"From Fleming?" Stevie asked.

Jade shrugged. "We could never prove it was him, but I always thought it was."

Stevie crossed her arms, her eyes fixed on the wall. "Well, well. I wonder where our Mr. Fleming is now." She reached for the phone and dialed police headquarters. She was eventually patched through to a downtown patrol sergeant and told him she wanted a 10-28 on Charles Fleming. If he was a licensed driver or had any sort of a criminal record, she would be able to pinpoint where he was. She gave the sergeant her cellular phone number.

"Tess, c'mon."

Tess followed Stevie downstairs, Jade on their heels.

"Where are you two going?" Jade asked, worry lines furrowing her forehead.

Stevie grabbed her jacket and stepped into her shoes. "See if we can find Roger Lemming. Don't worry, hon. I'll call you if we get him and bring him in."

*   *   *   *   *

Stevie drove straight to Lemming's house. This time his car was gone and there was no answer at the door. Either he sobered up in a matter of hours or he was out there drunk somewhere, Stevie told Tess.

"Bet you didn't think you'd end up working on your day off." Stevie winked at Tess from the driver's seat.

Tess grinned. "Hell, this is better than working patrol any day. I'd love to not have to write another traffic ticket again."

Stevie wasn't listening. She was wondering how someone like Roger Lemming could possibly have belonged to a group like the Moral Mercenaries. He used drugs and was promiscuous — hardly what she would have expected a zealous young redneck to evolve into.

The cellular phone rang. It was the patrol sergeant, and the news wasn't good. There was no record of a Charles Fleming that roughly matched the age of the man Stevie was looking for.

Stevie instructed the sergeant to issue a BOLO — be on the lookout for — to all units. She gave him a description of Roger Lemming, a description of his car, and the plate number. She explained that Lemming was non-arrestable, but that she wanted him detained until she got there because he was a material witness in a murder investigation.

Stevie cursed as she put the phone down.

"Where to next?" Tess asked eagerly.

Stevie frowned. "To Lemming's workplace on the off chance he's there."

They drove from Scarborough back downtown, to

the office building housing Hedley Enterprises. Stevie wondered idly what the name would be changed to. Would the company be sold? Or would Vanessa take the helm?

With an explanation and a flash of their badges, the building's security guard waved them on. But much to Stevie's chagrin, the place was empty.

She leaned against the corridor wall and sighed heavily. Back to square one.

CHAPTER TWELVE

Stevie and Tess had gone back to the house, having run out of ideas. They hadn't a clue where to find Roger Lemming. And that meant a frustrated Stevie was like a dog with a bur under its collar.

Pizza and a beer for supper had proved only a temporary distraction for Stevie, who kept glancing at the phone and willing it to ring with news on Lemming's whereabouts.

She felt better after the three of them took Tonka for a four-mile walk, Stevie's cellular phone clipped handily to her belt. Still no news.

Jade had chosen the video *The Jackal* in the hope that a fast-paced action movie would keep Stevie preoccupied. They'd been through this routine many times before, when Stevie was on the brink of solving a case, when all the loose ends finally began to fit together to form some kind of a hazy picture. It meant hours or sometimes days of a totally absorbed Stevie, who wavered, sometimes dramatically, between elation and frustration. To Jade, Stevie was like an apparition, not really there. She would race off, often without an explanation, she would toss and turn in bed, she wouldn't listen when spoken to, and she became forgetful around the house. And so Jade and Tonka would hold their breath until it was all over and another case was solved.

Jade and Tess carried most of the evening's conversation, Jade constantly teasing Tess about being too nervous to ask an acquaintance of Jade's out for a date.

Stevie stared glumly at the television screen, mentally trying to fit the pieces of the puzzle together. There were too many pieces missing, and she felt Andrew Myatt and Roger Lemming were the only ones who could fill in the holes. She grabbed her notebook from an end table and reached for the phone.

"Andrew Myatt?" Stevie said into the receiver, then identified herself. "I'm sorry to bother you on a Saturday evening, but I need to ask you some questions." It was obvious she was being met with some resistance, as she apologized again and firmly stated that if he didn't answer her questions on the phone, she'd come to his house.

Stevie plugged away, asking Myatt about his relationship with Roger Lemming. Had he seen Roger Lemming in recent years? Had he corresponded with him in any way? Could Lemming have been part of the blackmail scheme?

Stevie finally ended the brief phone call, every bit as frustrated as before she'd made the call.

"Well?" Jade and Tess asked in unison.

Stevie shook her head slowly, a sigh escaping her. "Hasn't seen or heard from Lemming since they graduated from university. And as far as he knows, Hedley was acting alone when he tried to blackmail him."

Tess leaned forward in her chair. "Maybe it's just a coincidence that Myatt and Lemming knew each other way back when and are both connected to this case."

"Yeah," Jade chimed in. "It's possible."

Stevie chewed on a fingernail. "And just a coincidence that James Hedley, who's Lemming's boss, is blackmailing Myatt? And that Hedley's wife, who once had an affair with Lemming, is now involved with Myatt's sister?" Stevie looked at them both. "I can't assume anything's a coincidence here. I do that, and this whole case could be down the toilet."

Stevie resorted to quiet contemplation again while Tess and Jade resumed the movie. The popcorn went mostly uneaten, and Stevie barely touched her beer. She wanted to be ready in case she got a call that Lemming was located. She barely watched the movie, and found herself wishing like hell that Jovanowski hadn't gone away for the weekend. She could use his ideas right now, not to mention his physical presence in case she would be interrogating Lemming later.

Better get used to it, her mind rattled. If

Jovanowski was true to his word and retired soon, she would be carrying the load anyway. She glanced at Tess, glad to have some help on hand.

"Honey," Stevie called to Jade. "Can I refill your wine?"

Jade was leaning forward on her elbows, her fingers steepled in front of her. She was staring, unblinking, at the television screen, as if in a trance.

"Jade?" Stevie asked, her tone quizzical.

Stevie noticed Jade's hands begin to tremble and her face to pale. She turned suddenly to Stevie, her eyes wide, a startled expression on her face. Her hand rose to her mouth and froze there.

"My god," she gasped.

Stevie was at her side in a flash, kneeling on the floor, while Tess stopped the movie.

"What is it, Jade?" Stevie asked, panic edging into her voice.

"It-it's Chuck," Jade stammered. "My assistant. Chuck O'Leary."

"What about him, honey?"

Jade dropped her hand into her lap. "It's him." Her voice was low, almost a whisper, but firm.

Tess said, "What are you talking about, Jade?"

Jade's eyes moved quickly between the two women. "It's *him*," she hissed. "Chuck O'Leary is Charles Fleming! It's just dawned on me, watching this movie with disguises and stuff. I mean, he looks different now, with his hair short and balding and . . . he must have contact lenses or something."

Stevie forced herself to stay calm even though her thoughts were already racing. "Are you sure about this?"

Jade nodded as Stevie took her hand. "Yes, I'm sure. And he's creepy and watching me and stuff, just like he used to back in school."

Stevie stood up and walked to the phone. "He's obviously changed his name."

Tess stood too. "Are you calling to get a ten-twenty-eight on him?"

Stevie nodded, then quickly put the receiver back in its cradle. She looked at Tess. "No. If I do that, they'll give me his address. I'd rather go to the coroner's office and have Jade dig up his address."

Tess looked perplexed. "But it'd be faster to just phone and —"

"I know," Stevie said, cutting her off. "But I want the chance to look around O'Leary's office. I don't want to have to wait until Monday and beg for a search warrant. This way, if I'm already on the premises under the guise of looking for his address, it's an in for us." She looked at Jade. "Can you get us in there?"

"Of course," Jade answered.

Stevie picked up her cellular phone. "Once we have the address of O'Leary or Fleming or whoever the hell he is, and take a look around, we'll head over to his house to interview him. Let's go, gang."

The Ontario Coroner's Office was a brown brick structure on Grosvenor Street, right beside the much taller, gray granite Center of Forensic Sciences. Women's College Hospital was just down the street. The buildings were all nondescript, and the business of death and sickness and crime would hardly go noticed if not for the street's steady stream of police cars, ambulances, and hearses.

At night, the streetscape struck Stevie as eerily quiet, peaceful and almost reassuring that all was right in the world. Except Stevie knew firsthand that wasn't true. She knew the dark secrets these buildings contained, the remnants of a sometimes sick and twisted segment of society. Remnants that would be put under microscopes, picked apart and studied by people like Jade and herself. It was that meticulous analysis that helped keep the streets safe and helped put some kind of order and understanding to an otherwise disorderly and nonsensical incident.

Jade got them in with her electronic key card. They got as far as the security guard's desk, where they stopped and identified themselves. Jade spun a story about needing to pick up some paperwork. With that, they were soon upstairs in a receptionist's office, where Jade knew personnel files were kept.

Jade pulled on a file cabinet drawer. "Shit, it's locked."

Stevie leaned against the uncooperative metal cabinet. "What about the computers? There must be an electronic list of employees' home addresses."

Jade was already out the door and down the hall, heading to her office. "I should be able to access it from my machine," she called over her shoulder.

Stevie and Tess rushed to catch up.

"It's just that his whole file could have told us more about his personal history, dammit." Jade switched her computer on, then began tapping the keyboard.

"We can get a warrant for his file anyway," Stevie

reassured Jade. "Don't forget, I want to take a look around his office or wherever he spends his time when he's not in the morgue."

Jade nodded and silently continued her search. "Bingo," she finally said and pointed to the monitor. "There's his address."

Stevie committed it to memory. "Good, now where's his office?"

Jade led them down to the basement, which immediately produced sour faces from Tess and Stevie, who knew the autopsy suites and the huge refrigerated storage area were down there.

Tess looked as pale as a fresh blanket of snow. "Do we really have to be down here at night? Maybe I can wait upstairs."

Stevie laughed. "No way, girl. If I have to be down here, you can be down here too. And yeah, it's an order. Don't forget," she winked, "I am a ranking officer."

Tess scowled and trudged behind, following them into a large room separated into cubicles by five-foot-high dividers.

Jade spread her arm out. "This is where the assistants work. They each get a cubicle."

"Where's O'Leary's?" Stevie asked.

Jade led them to the far corner of the room. The cubicle was small, containing only a desk, a chair, and a large filing cabinet. O'Leary's work area was tidy.

Stevie opened each desk drawer, one at a time, and quickly rifled through them.

Tess leaned over Stevie's shoulder. "What exactly are you looking for?"

Stevie shrugged. "Beats me. Anything that might tell us a little more about him."

There wasn't much of interest. A dry-cleaning bill, a Visa statement, and the rest was all work related.

Stevie turned her attention to the large filing cabinet and was relieved to find it wasn't locked. The metal cabinet was old and didn't even contain any sort of locking device. She started at the top and flipped through file folders without having to remove any. She didn't want to leave any obvious signs that she'd been there.

The second and third drawers were just as innocuous as the first — more notes on autopsies, research articles, and policy papers.

Stevie pulled out the final, bottom drawer, metal scraping on metal, the grinding squeal like fingernails on a chalkboard. She flipped through the folders until she came across one that contained newsletters from an American group, the Moral Majority. The next file folder contained newsletters from an even more disturbing group — an antiabortion organization that promoted terrorist-like activities.

Stevie whistled, passing one of the newsletters to Tess. "This idiot obviously didn't leave his Moral Mercenary days far behind." Still on her knees, she bent over the open drawer again and dug her hand into the very back of the deep drawer. She froze there, a quizzical expression on her face that prompted Tess and Jade to hang over her shoulder, trying to peer in.

Stevie took a tiny, pen-size flashlight from her jacket pocket, shoved her head into the drawer and shone the light into what her hand had earlier touched.

A smile spread across her face. "Well, well, what have we here." She pulled a mass of blond hair from the compartment.

Tess and Jade gasped collectively at the wig Stevie held up.

Stevie, still smiling triumphantly, said, "I'll bet you a week's pay a strand from this wig will match up with the synthetic hair found in Hedley's bedroom."

Stevie dug her hand back in the drawer and pulled out a dark blue dress. "Boy, it just keeps getting better and better."

It was Jade's turn to go pale. "My god, he killed James Hedley? Why?"

"I don't know," Stevie answered impatiently. "But we'll find out. O'Leary certainly had the know-how to inject Hedley with a fatal dose of drugs, and obviously had the means." She shook the wig. "Honey," she said hurriedly to Jade. "I need a paper bag for this stuff to take in as evidence. Can you do that for me?"

"Of course," Jade answered absently, still shaking her head.

Stevie, Jade, and Tess had just climbed into Stevie's Mustang when Stevie's cellular phone rang. She nearly dropped it in her haste to hit the answer button.

"Houston here," she finally said into the phone. She listened and instructed the caller to keep the unit at the location.

"What's going on?" Jade asked, the car tires squealing as the powerful turbo engine leapt to life.

"They've found Lemming's car."

"Where?" Tess piped up.

Stevie stepped on the gas again, causing her passengers to jerk forward in their seats. "In front of Vanessa's house."

"Shit!" Tess cursed.

"I know," Stevie agreed. "But let's all just remain

calm. A two-man unit is there and will wait outside until we get there. They won't let Lemming leave."

Jade was biting her nails. "What the hell would he be doing at Vanessa's?"

Stevie sighed. "I don't know, but I doubt they're having a tea party."

Tess, who was in the back seat, leaned forward. "What about this O'Leary creep?"

Stevie rounded a corner sharply. "He'll have to wait."

The drive to the north end of the city took them only fifteen minutes, the scenery changing from high-rise apartment buildings and narrow houses plopped down on meager lots, to wide and well-manicured lawns with extravagant, colonial and Victorian-style homes. Stevie had elected not to make a pit stop at her office to pick up her gun and handcuffs. With two uniformed officers at Vanessa's house, she was sure they could handle Roger Lemming, even if he did become unruly.

Stevie pulled up in front of the familiar Roxborough Drive address of Vanessa Hedley. Sure enough, Roger Lemming's BMW was parked on the street in front, and Stevie zipped in behind it. She said a silent prayer of thanks that the patrol car had stayed at a discreet distance. She didn't want Lemming tipped off just yet.

Climbing out of her car, Stevie motioned to the uniformed officers to come with her. Tess and Jade climbed out too, but Jade got only halfway out of the car before Stevie's hand firmly grasped her shoulder.

"Jade," Stevie said brusquely. "I want you to stay in the car, and I mean that."

True to her nature, Jade protested. "Why do I have to stay in the car?"

Stevie's grip tightened. "Jade, I don't have time to argue. Just get in the car, now." Her tone was firm and scolding and left little room for argument. It was exactly the way she'd spoken her entire career to some- one who was causing trouble, someone whom she needed to control immediately. She wanted no repeat performance of her first murder case, where Jade's spontaneous actions had nearly gotten her killed.

Jade complied with a face that said they'd talk about this later.

Tess smiled at the two officers, who were from her own division. "Hey Jack, Tony."

"Tess," ordered Stevie, who was the commanding officer on the scene. "You and Tony take the back door." Stevie turned to appraise the hulking officer behind her, who looked more like an Arnold, as in Schwarzenegger, than a Jack. "Jack, I'm Stevie Houston, by the way. C'mon with me."

Stevie cut him off as he was about to speak. "We'll knock first, identify ourselves, and if no one lets us in, we're going in anyway."

They strode to the porch, the young officer staring wide-eyed at Stevie, as though she were some alien from outer space. She knocked hard on the door, shouted out it was the police, and got no response. The door was locked.

"Can you break this thing down?" Stevie asked him hopefully.

Jack pressed his palms against the door, gave it a light shrug, and shook his massive head. "Solid oak.

Only a battering ram is going to get through this thing."

"Can I have your flashlight?"

He shrugged and handed Stevie the heavy steel flashlight.

Holding the flashlight out like it was a knife, she stabbed at the narrow window that ran along the length of the door, punching a hole in the glass. Tiny shards of the glass tinkled to the ceramic floor inside. Stevie gouged at the hole with the flashlight until it was big enough to put her hand through it to unlock the door from the inside.

Jack, Stevie finally noticed, was working his mouth but nothing was coming out.

"Don't worry," she whispered. "I have probable cause to believe someone's life is in danger. Radio Tess and your partner and tell them we'll come through and let them in." Stevie knew she might be stretching it in what she'd told the officer. But then again, maybe not.

Stevie turned the door handle and opened the door as quietly as she could while Jack did as she'd told him. The house was dark and eerily quiet. Stevie felt the hair on the back of her neck prickle. They were here: Vanessa and Lemming.

Quietly the four police congregated in a hallway, Stevie directing each with hand signals to search the main floor and the basement. Stevie took the kitchen and dining room, searching each closet and even the lower cupboards of the kitchen. Minutes later, the four gathered at the foot of the staircase leading to the upper floor. None of them had found anything.

"Jack," Stevie whispered to the hulking officer.

"You stay at the foot of these stairs. No one gets by you, got that?"

He nodded.

Stevie looked at Tess and Tony. "You guys come with me."

Quietly, the three jogged up the thickly carpeted stairs, Stevie leading the way, the flashlight still in her hand. They could hear nothing but their own breathing.

Stevie tapped Tess on the shoulder and nodded toward the master bedroom, where light faintly escaped through the crack at the bottom of the door. In a move they had all practiced since they were recruits, Stevie and Tony stood to one side of the door, Tony crouched with his gun drawn, while Tess stood ready on the other side.

With a nod from Stevie, Tess booted the door in and Tony swung into position.

"Police! Freeze!" Stevie yelled out, moving in behind Tony.

As the three of them swept into the room, they heard a gasp, and they all noticed Vanessa at the same moment. She sat in a wooden chair at a desk, her hands and feet bound, duct tape over her mouth.

Stevie's discerning glance swept over Vanessa, taking in the information faster than her mind could process it. There was a piece of paper on the desk, a syringe. Vanessa's eyes were large red orbs, and her cheeks bulged as she tried to speak, the muffled groans and noises more frantic by the second. Her gaze kept jumping to the double doors of the closet on the far wall.

Stevie turned just as the doors exploded open and

two figures crashed through. She felt as though she were frozen in place, like a bad dream where everything was rushing around her and she couldn't catch up. It seemed like minutes before her free hand reached for her gun; she'd forgotten it wasn't there.

One of the figures barreled into Tess, sending her backward into the wall before he ran through the doorway. It was Roger Lemming, Stevie recognized. *Fast.* The word popped into her mind. Lemming was faster on his feet than she would have guessed, and it startled her that she should be thinking and not acting. She shoved Tony in the direction Lemming was fleeing, then heard the crash at the bottom of the stairs. She knew Jack wouldn't let Lemming by.

The other figure had run to the large bedroom window.

"O'Leary!" Stevie yelled out. "Stay where you are. Don't move!"

None of them moved for a moment: O'Leary at the windows, Stevie near the bed, Tess on her hands and knees near the door. It was a standoff to see who would move first.

O'Leary, his beady little eyes moving rapidly from Stevie to Tess, turned his back to them. In one swift, arching motion, he picked up a chair and tossed it through the window.

Stevie was diving across the bed just as the glass shattered.

"You little son-of-a bitch," she cursed. But it was too late. He was already gone.

Tess, too, was gone by the time Stevie turned back for the door. Tess was sprinting down the stairs.

Stevie followed as fast her legs would carry her, but Tess was already out the front door by the time Stevie reached the bottom of the stairs.

"What's going on?" Tony asked Stevie as she sprinted by. "She just grabbed my radio and took off."

Stevie barely slowed down. "You guys stay with the prisoner. Get us some backup."

She stopped on the porch and scanned the dark street, finally seeing the tail end of Tess as she ran through a neighbor's driveway. Stevie gave chase, wishing she'd taken the two-way radio from Jack so she could communicate with Tess. She suddenly had a new appreciation for wearing a uniform and all the handy accouterments that went with it.

Tess was a good runner, but so was Stevie. It wasn't long before she'd narrowed the gap between them. Tess would scamper over a fence, then Stevie would. Tess would hurdle a garbage can. So would Stevie. They communicated with hand signals, and Stevie knew O'Leary wasn't far ahead of them. Dogs barked with each yard they passed through. Motion lights fastened on the backs of houses or on garages clicked on as they scampered by.

Tess hopped another chain-link fence. Only this time, she landed face down with a thud.

"Fuck!" Tess swore, pulling her boot free of the fence.

Stevie hopped the same fence. "Are you okay, Tess?"

Tess began to haul herself up and pointed. "Keep going."

Stevie followed in the direction of a new round of

dogs barking and a new stream of backyard motion lights. She was astounded O'Leary hadn't hurt himself back at the house, jumping through the window, onto the porch roof, and then to the ground. The little twerp should at least have a broken ankle, she thought to herself. Tess probably did, and all she'd done was jump over a four-foot fence.

Stevie was getting damn tired of running. Fitness wasn't exactly her hobby. Her ears were pounding, her lungs were on fire, and her legs were starting to cramp. She stopped in the shadow of a tree to listen and look around. A movement behind a hedge not more than a hundred feet away was so slight, Stevie almost thought she had imagined it. But there was no wind tonight, not even a breeze. The movement was manmade.

Stevie dropped to her hands and knees and crawled toward the hedge as fast as she could, the metal flashlight still clamped in her fist. She'd forgotten about it until now. The dew-soaked grass was soaking her knees, but the slipperiness allowed her to go faster. It was almost like gliding on ice.

O'Leary, Stevie knew, was behind the six-foot hedge, and her eyes followed his slow movement down the length of it. He was trying to get to the street, where perhaps he had a getaway car parked, for all Stevie knew. She would have to close in on him before he got there and made a fresh break for it.

Stevie was just a few feet from O'Leary now, with only the thick hedge separating them. She could faintly hear his heavy breathing as she struggled to stifle her own. There were only a few feet left of the hedge, and Stevie crawled faster, staying low, staying quiet. She was at the edge of it, just ahead of O'Leary, when she pulled herself up to a crouch position. She'd never played football, but she was sure she was ready to make the tackle. She just hoped O'Leary didn't know how to play football.

He stepped out and Stevie lunged, all one-hundred-and-seventy pounds of her landing full force on the diminutive O'Leary. She squashed him like a bug, splaying him out like he'd been pinned onto a board. He squirmed and writhed like he was fighting for his life, and it took all of Stevie's strength to keep him there.

"You're under arrest," she told him in ragged breaths as she struggled to keep him under her. She read him his rights, as though his capture was now a fait accompli. He groaned and sputtered and bucked, until finally Stevie landed a hard crack between his shoulder blades with her trusty flashlight. He yelped, his body sagging from the pain.

"You got him!" It was Tess, hobbling over to Stevie as fast as she could. "I've radioed our position. A unit's on the way."

Stevie was still sitting on O'Leary, his arms painfully twisted behind his back like a Gumby figure, his face kissing the wet grass.

"You wouldn't happen to have any handcuffs, would you?" Stevie asked hopelessly.

"Sorry, fresh out today," Tess replied. She sat down on O'Leary's legs to insure he wouldn't be going anywhere until they were good and ready to move him.

"You know," Tess said, a smile erasing the pain on her face. "I could get used to working with you."

Stevie laughed. "You should know that I'm hard on

my partners. Ted had a heart attack on our first case. And now you with your ankle!"

"That might be true, Stevie, but at least your partners always show up."

Stevie nodded and couldn't help but reflect on Jovanowski's absence. He was gone, she knew. Their partnership was over.

EPILOGUE

Stevie put her feet up on the coffee table, the *Sunday Star* folded neatly on her lap, a steaming cup of coffee in her fist, the dog curled up asleep on the floor. It was how she loved spending her Sunday mornings. She could see from out the windows that the leaves were starting to turn color. It was October, and soon enough November's gray skies and damp, chilly temperatures would permeate the city. Stevie hated early winter, and thinking about what lay ahead always prevented her from enjoying the bright, mild, and colorful fall season.

The doorbell rang. Tonka let out the obligatory bark but had no intention of leaving her sunny spot in front of the window.

"Oh, you brave watchdog," Stevie teased her, and Tonka's ears wilted as though in shame.

Jade scurried out of the kitchen where she had begun to thaw a roast. "I'll get it."

"Hi, Ted," Stevie heard Jade say. It was Jovanowski, and Stevie could hear him mumbling his apologies for stopping in unannounced.

"Nonsense," Jade replied. "C'mon in and have a cup of coffee with us."

Stevie rose from her chair, her coffee still in her hand, and greeted her partner in the hallway. "Where's Jocelyn? Should have brought her too. It's been weeks since we've seen you two together."

Jade laughed. "Are you sure you haven't dumped her and aren't just pretending you're still together?"

Jovanowski gave them a look that said they were both crazy, then rolled his eyes. "She's house hunting."

"Let me guess," Stevie grinned. "You didn't want to go so you said you had important business to discuss with me, right?"

Jovanowski shook his head in defeat. "You know me too well, Tex. Almost like we were married or something."

"Now that's a scary thought," Stevie laughed.

"Damn right it is," Jovanowski barked.

Jade led the way to the kitchen and poured a cup of black coffee for Jovanowski. "Have a seat, Ted."

Stevie and Jovanowski sat in the wicker stools at the kitchen island while Jade began to prepare another pot for the coffee maker.

"So," Stevie began carefully, knowing how private Jovanowski could be. "You two getting ready to make the big move?"

Jovanowski nodded, his beefy hands clamped around his coffee mug like it was his security blanket. He shifted in his seat, his eyes taking on a sheen of excitement. "That was great the way that Hedley case came together, wasn't it?"

Stevie knew there was a reason he was changing the subject. She went with the flow. "Sure was," she agreed.

Jovanowski shook his head in wonder, his smile full of pride. "You hit a solo home run with this one, kid."

Stevie began to protest, but Jovanowski held up his hand. "No really, you did. I mean, I was only around for some of the leg work, and I was still figuring it was Vanessa behind the murder, the blackmail, the whole thing. But not you, you had it pegged."

Stevie's smile was rueful. She knew where this conversation was going. "It only came together at the last second. I didn't even know O'Leary and Lemming were in on it together until we found them at the house."

Jade stood on the other side of the island, resting her elbows on the ceramic surface. "Vanessa sure owes her life to you, hon. If you and Tess hadn't walked in when you did, she'd be dead right now of the same type of overdose that killed her husband."

Stevie had already spent a couple of sleepless nights contemplating what might have happened if they'd been a few more minutes later in getting to Vanessa. O'Leary and Fleming were going to force her to write a suicide note confessing to blackmailing Andrew Myatt along with her husband, then killing her husband when he didn't press harder for a deal. O'Leary was then going to stick her with a needle, the same way he'd injected James Hedley with a deadly combination of heroin and cocaine.

"Well," Stevie exhaled contentedly. "I feel totally ready for their preliminary trial tomorrow. Those two sickos are going to the pen."

Jovanowski nodded. "O'Leary is definitely a sicko. The streets will be a lot safer with that little weasel off them. Vancouver's sending a team here this week to take a look at him. They figure he might have had a hand in bombing an abortion clinic a couple of years back."

"Is that why he changed his last name?" Jade asked.

Jovanowski swallowed a mouthful of coffee. "Probably. I figure that guy's got quite a track record if we dig deep enough. Lemming, on the other hand, is just a bum. The guy'd do anything for a buck."

Stevie drummed her fingers on the counter, her eyes fixed on a tiny, distant speck of egg stuck to the stovetop. "Not surprising he was in with Hedley on blackmailing the Myatts for half the take. When Myatt didn't bite, he went to Plan B because he was so desperate for money."

Jade's eyebrows quirked. "Plan B?"

Stevie had been so busy with paperwork the past week, she hadn't filled Jade in on every aspect. "Plan B was to get rid of Hedley. See, we found this contract he had with Hedley. If Hedley died, Lemming would become the largest minority shareholder of the company, with Vanessa holding the slight majority after inheriting her husband's share. But if Vanessa died or became incarcerated and couldn't sit on the board, then Lemming effectively took over ownership of the company."

Jade nodded appreciatively. "So that's why they first tried to frame Vanessa for her husband's murder. And when that didn't work, they decided to go for the kill."

"Bingo," Ted remarked. "And Lemming was sure he could make that company a top performer, unlike Hedley had been able to do."

Jade looked puzzled again. "How did he get Chuck O'Leary involved? I mean, I know they were buddies in school, but I don't understand why Chuck would do this."

Stevie's smile was that of a cynic, of someone who'd seen every kind of nut out there. "O'Leary's the type who's just looking for violence with any kind of moral justification in his little pea brain. Of course, he would get a small chunk of change for his effort, but it's the thrill of killing that gets that guy off."

Jovanowski began tapping his mug with the chunky gold ring on his right hand. It made a high-pitched clinking sound. "I don't think it took much to convince O'Leary that the world would be a better place without James Hedley in it. Vanessa, for that matter, too."

Jade sighed. "He certainly hated her when he found out a long time ago that she and I were having an affair. I don't imagine I'm a popular person in his book either. I guess he set that fire in the morgue on purpose so my autopsy notes would be ruined."

"I'm just glad Stevie cracked this case when she did," Jovanowski said to Jade. "Who knows, you could have been his next target."

Stevie bristled at the thought that Jade had spent weeks working with that psycho O'Leary. "Anyway, they'll both be off the street for a long time. Maybe Vanessa can finally find some peace in her life with Cheryl Myatt."

Jade sighed. "I don't know if Vanessa has it in her to be happy."

Jovanowski loudly sipped his coffee.

"Speaking of happy," Stevie piped up. "I'm glad to hear you and Jocelyn are moving in together. Does this mean you're getting married?"

Jovanowski shot her a menacing glare. "This cat ain't walking down the aisle again."

Jade, a fellow Roman Catholic, wagged her finger at Jovanowski. "Living in sin!" she gasped teasingly.

"Oh yeah, like you should talk," Jovanowski smirked. "I don't see Stevie dragging you down no aisle."

Jade reached across the counter and touched Stevie's hand. "Believe me, I'd be dragging *her* down the aisle if we could legally get married."

Jovanowski blushed, as he always did when Jade and Stevie became affectionate in his company, or talked intimately about their relationship. They knew he loved them both and respected their relationship. He just didn't like to be confronted with it.

"Stevie," he said, eyeing her cautiously. "I came here to tell you it's official. I'm retiring next month."

Stevie had been waiting for this shoe to drop. And now that it had dropped, she felt scared, alone, like a kid kicked out on her own. She felt her stomach tighten into a knot. "Are you sure about this?" she whispered, afraid she'd choke up if she spoke any louder.

Jovanowski nodded solemnly, staring into his near-empty cup. "I'm old, Stevie. I'm tired. I'm not the detective I used to be." When he looked up at her, his eyes were moist. "I know you'd do the same if you were me."

Stevie could do nothing but nod her agreement. She too, someday, if she lived long enough, would have to defer to her younger comrades. She just hoped she knew when it was time to step down, the way Jovanowski seemed to know. She figured it must be like an aging professional athlete, who knows that with each match or game, they're losing a bit more of their edge. The hard part was having the courage to step back, to throw in the towel.

"And," Jovanowski continued, "your friend Tess has made quite of an impression on the inspector. He's going to talk to her superiors, put in a good word for her."

Stevie brightened. "Does that mean they'll move her to homicide?

"Not yet," Jovanowski answered. "They'll want her to spend at least a year in sex crimes or fraud or something. But yeah, she's got a future in homicide if she wants one. And I know just the teacher for her."

He winked at Stevie, and she felt her confidence soar. She leaned over and kissed him on the cheek.

"What's that for?" he asked, surprised.

Stevie shrugged. "For being *my* teacher. I couldn't have asked for any better."

A few of the publications of
THE NAIAD PRESS, INC.
P.O. Box 10543   Tallahassee, Florida 32302
Phone (850) 539-5965
Toll-Free Order Number: 1-800-533-1973
Web Site: WWW.NAIADPRESS.COM
Mail orders welcome. Please include 15% postage.
Write or call for our free catalog which also features an
incredible selection of lesbian videos.